THE RAINBOW magic

PARTY FAIRIES TREASURY

Special thanks to
Narinder Dhami,
Sue Mongredien
and Marilyn Kaye

ORCHARD BOOKS
338 Euston Road, London NW1 3BH
Orchard Books Australia
Level 17/207 Kent Street, Sydney, NSW 2000

First published as an abridged version by Orchard Books in 2010.

A CIP catalogue record for this book is available
from the British Library.

ISBN 978 1 40830 914 8

1 3 5 7 9 10 8 6 4 2

Printed in China
Orchard Books is a division of Hachette Children's Books,
an Hachette UK company

www.hachette.co.uk

The RAINBOW magic

PARTY FAIRIES Treasury

by Daisy Meadows

Illustrated by Georgie Ripper

ORCHARD BOOKS

The Fairyland Palace

Clearing

The Village Hall

Twisty Lane

Our gracious king and gentle queen
Are loved by fairies all.
One thousand years have they ruled well,
Through troubles great and small.

In honour of their glorious reign
A party has been planned,
To celebrate their jubilee
Throughout all Fairyland.

The party is a royal surprise,
We hope they'll be delighted.
So shine your wand and press your dress...
For you have been invited!

RSVP: HRH The Fairy Godmother

Contents

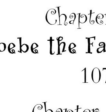

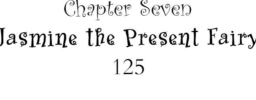

Cherry the Cake Fairy

Chapter One

Cherry the Cake Fairy

"I just know this is going to be a wonderful birthday!" Kirsty Tate exclaimed happily, her eyes shining.

Mrs Tate laughed across the breakfast table. "You've only been awake for half an hour, Kirsty," she said.

"I know," Kirsty replied. "But look at all these cards I've been sent! And there's my party this afternoon. And best of all, Rachel's here for a whole week!" She grinned at her best friend, Rachel Walker, who was sitting next to her. The two girls were spending a week of the Easter holidays together. They had met on holiday the year before and, since then, they had had all kinds of magical Fairyland adventures together.

The girls finished their breakfast and went to get dressed. Rachel was halfway up the stairs behind Kirsty, when she noticed another envelope coming through the letterbox. It was a very grand-looking, sparkly gold envelope, and it felt heavy in her hand. She glanced at

the front curiously – and then
gasped in surprise.

Miss Kirsty Tate and *Miss Rachel
Walker*, the beautiful loopy
handwriting read.

She raced up the stairs,
two at a time, puzzling it over.
She didn't recognise the handwriting,
so it couldn't be from her mum or dad.

But who else knew that she was staying
with Kirsty?

"Look," cried Rachel, bursting into
Kirsty's bedroom. "Another card –
and it's for both of us!"

Kirsty took the envelope and
gently turned it over. "You open
it," she said,
passing the
letter back
to Rachel.

Rachel's fingers trembled with
excitement as she carefully broke
the wax seal. As soon as the
envelope was open, glittering
clouds of fairy dust billowed into
the air, followed by a rainbow of
colour that soared across the room.

Both girls stared, open-mouthed. Riding on top of the rainbow, just as if he was surfing on a wave, was Bertram, the Fairyland frog footman!

Bertram hopped off the rainbow onto Kirsty's chest of drawers and tooted on a bugle. Then he pulled a

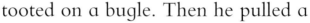

tiny scroll from one of his pockets and unrolled it. "Ahem. It is with great pleasure," he began, "that I bring you good news. The Fairy Godmother hereby invites Kirsty Tate and Rachel Walker to a surprise party – for the Fairy king and queen's 1000th jubilee!"

"Wow!" gasped Rachel.

From another of his pockets, Bertram pulled out a tiny bag of fairy dust and

began sprinkling it over Kirsty's mirror. As the girls watched, the mirror's reflection vanished and a whole new scene appeared before their eyes.

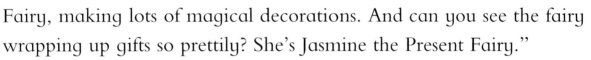

"It's Fairyland!" Rachel breathed, leaning closer for a better look.

"Correct," said Bertram. "The Fairy Party Workshop, to be precise. All the Party Fairies have been working very hard to make sure the king and queen's party is absolutely perfect. There's Cherry the Cake Fairy, making a special party cake," Bertram told them, pointing a webbed green finger. "That's Grace the Glitter Fairy, making lots of magical decorations. And can you see the fairy wrapping up gifts so prettily? She's Jasmine the Present Fairy."

The two girls watched in delight as Jasmine tied a pink satin bow around one of the presents.

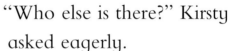

"Who else is there?" Kirsty asked eagerly.

Bertram pointed. "There's Polly the Party Fun Fairy. She's in charge of party games. And Melodie the Music Fairy sorts out the best party tunes."

The girls fell silent and listened to the sweet sounds of fairy music tinkling through the mirror.

"It's gorgeous," Rachel sighed.

Bertram went on. "Honey the Sweet Fairy is making sure there are enough treats to go round, and Phoebe the Fashion Fairy — she's the one with the extra-sparkly wings, look — is in charge of everybody's party outfits."

Kirsty gazed in wonder, her eyes wide with excitement. "And we're really invited to the party?"

"Oh, yes," Bertram replied.

"So, when is it? And how will we get there?" asked Kirsty.

Bertram murmured something at the mirror and the Fairyland scene dissolved into hundreds of twinkling stars, before finally

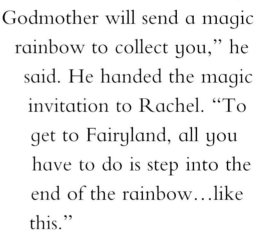

disappearing. "The party's at the end of the week. And the Fairy Godmother will send a magic rainbow to collect you," he said. He handed the magic invitation to Rachel. "To get to Fairyland, all you have to do is step into the end of the rainbow…like this."

Kirsty and Rachel watched as Bertram placed one froggy foot, then another, into the colourful rainbow that hovered in the air.

And then - whoosh - with a shower of golden fairy dust, he was gone.

Rachel and Kirsty got dressed, chatting excitedly.

"I can't wait to go to Fairyland again," Kirsty grinned, brushing her hair.

Just then, there was a shout from downstairs. "Come on, girls!" Mrs Tate called. "There's lots to do before the party starts."

Kirsty chuckled. " Do you know, I'd almost forgotten all about my party!"

The girls laughed and hurried downstairs. In the kitchen, Mr Tate was icing Kirsty's birthday cake. "There," he said, putting nine candles on top. "It's all finished."

"That looks delicious, Dad," Kirsty said, hugging him. "Come on, Rachel – let's see what Mum wants us to do."

Mrs Tate soon had the two girls making up party bags for all of Kirsty's guests. Then they blew up lots of pink and lilac balloons to hang from the ceiling. And finally there was just time for the girls to put on their party dresses before the guests arrived.

"Musical Statues first," Mrs Tate announced to all the girls gathered in the lounge. "When the music stops – so do you!"

The music started and everybody danced. Then Mr Tate switched it off – and everybody froze on the spot. Rachel was standing on one leg, trying to keep as still as possible, when she suddenly saw swirls of red and purple glitter floating through the doorway. She stared in surprise, wondering what it could be. Kirsty's startled expression told Rachel that she had spotted the glitter too, but none of the other children seemed to have noticed anything unusual.

The sparkling dust floated up to Rachel, drifting right under her nose. "Atishoo! Atishoo! Atishoo!" she sneezed.

Now the dust was under Kirsty's nose, too. It was so ticklish, she just couldn't help rubbing her nose.

"Rachel and Kirsty – you two are out!" Mrs Tate said. "Here comes the music again."

As quickly as they had appeared, the swirls of red and purple glitter vanished.

Kirsty grabbed Rachel's arm and pointed towards the door.

Rachel followed Kirsty's finger, and a broad smile spread over her face. For there, hovering in mid-air and waving at the girls, was a tiny sparkling fairy!

"You're one of the Party Fairies!" Rachel exclaimed as they rushed over to speak to the fairy. "We saw you in Bertram's picture."

The fairy smiled. She had lovely, deep violet eyes and long, dark, curly hair, tied in bunches with red ribbons. She wore a red skirt, a pink wrap-around top, red party shoes and stripy socks. From her wrist, swung a sparkly red party bag.

"I certainly am," she replied, with a little curtsey. "I'm Cherry the Cake Fairy." An anxious frown creased her forehead. "I'm sorry if my fairy dust spoiled your game," she went on, "but I really need your help!"

"Of course!" Kirsty said at once.

"Whatever's happened?" Rachel asked.

Cherry smiled gratefully. "Well, you see, as the Cake Fairy, whenever a party is in danger of being ruined by a spoiled cake, I get called away from Fairyland to fix it. And today, I've been very busy. One of Jack Frost's goblins has been spoiling birthday cakes all over the country." She bit her lip. "And he's on his way to Kirsty's party right now!"

17

Rachel's mouth fell open.

Kirsty glanced over to the kitchen door. "Why is the goblin spoiling all the cakes?" she asked. "And what can we do to stop him?"

Cherry's eyes flashed. "Nobody knows what the goblin is up to," she told the girls. "But one thing's for sure – if Jack Frost's behind it, it's bound to be something bad." She shrugged. "All we can do is try to catch the goblin before he causes any more trouble."

"What are we waiting for?" Rachel cried. "Let's stand guard over Kirsty's cake at once!"

The girls raced to the kitchen, with Cherry fluttering along behind. As soon as they opened the kitchen door, though, they knew that they were too late. All the candles had been pulled out of Kirsty's cake, and there were goblin footprints in the icing.

"Oh, no!" cried Kirsty in dismay. "He's ruined it!"

"He's taken all the candles, too," Rachel added crossly.

"And I'll take this, as well!" they heard somebody cackle. And before anyone could stop him, a grinning green goblin jumped out from behind one of the table legs, snatched Cherry's party bag out of her hands and ran off, laughing nastily.

"Hey!" Cherry cried. "Give that back. We've got to get my

party bag back!" Cherry cried, flying after the thief. "Quick!"

The goblin was just about to dodge out of the kitchen door, when Pearl came bounding into the room. As soon as Kirsty's kitten saw the goblin, she fluffed up her black and white fur in alarm and hissed.

The goblin's eyes bulged in panic and he skidded to a halt. Then he climbed up to one of the kitchen cupboards and locked himself in!

Cherry flitted about anxiously. "That party bag has got all my magical fairy dust inside," she fretted. "I need that to help make parties perfect – and to finish off the king and queen's jubilee cake."

Rachel banged on the cupboard door. "Give that party bag back to Cherry this minute!" she ordered the goblin.

"No chance," the goblin shouted back sulkily. "It's mine now – and as soon as I get out of here, I'll be giving it to Jack Frost."

"What does he want it for?" Kirsty asked curiously.

The goblin gave a gloating chuckle. "For his party of course," he replied. "The king and queen said he's got to stay in his ice castle, but they didn't say he couldn't have a party – and a very grand one it's going to be, too! Now that I've got this party bag of magic dust, his cake is going to be the most splendid cake you ever saw." There was another cackle of glee from the cupboard. "Just you wait – once we've got all the Party Fairies' party bags, Jack Frost will use the magic dust, instead of his own magic, to make his party extra-special."

Cherry had turned quite pale. She beckoned the girls back over to the table, where they huddled together to hear her whisper. "It's bad enough that he's got my party bag when I haven't finished the king and queen's cake," she said. "But if the goblins are planning to steal all the magical party bags, then none of the Party Fairies will be able to finish their work in time for the jubilee." She shook her head miserably. "The surprise party will be ruined!"

The girls thought hard to try and find a way of recovering Cherry's party bag. But they couldn't think of anything.

"The Fairy Godmother is much more powerful than a goblin," Cherry sighed. "She'd soon sort all this out if only I could get the goblin back to Fairyland. But I can't magic him there while he's in that cupboard. I need him to keep still, so that I can wave my wand over him."

Kirsty found her gaze drifting towards her ruined birthday cake. "Poor Dad spent ages on that icing," she said sadly. Then she grinned suddenly as a thought struck her. "That's it!" she muttered. "That's how we'll catch him!"

Quickly, she took out a box of icing sugar and started mixing some icing in a bowl. Then she added quietly, "Cherry, could you use some fairy magic to make this icing extra-sticky?"

"No problem," Cherry replied. She waved her wand over the bowl. The pink icing glittered for a split-second and strange red and purple sparks crackled above it. Then it turned a glossy pink again.

"It's a trap!" she whispered to Rachel and Cherry as she covered the cake with the new icing. "Let's leave the cake here on the table and get back to the party." she announced loudly.

Holding their breath, Rachel and Cherry followed Kirsty out of the room and waited outside to see if Kirsty's trap would work.

21

Sure enough, after a moment, the cupboard door creaked open and the goblin climbed down and skipped gleefully across the floor. Grinning nastily, he climbed up onto the kitchen table, and then made a massive leap straight onto the top of the newly-iced cake when suddenly...

"I'm stuck!" the goblin howled.

"Good!" Cherry flew over to the goblin, her eyes on her precious party bag. "And now I'm going to send us all to Fairyland. Once I've got my party bag back, I can magic Kirsty the most beautiful birthday cake you've ever seen."

"But what about the party?" Rachel pointed out. "Musical Statues must be about to end soon."

Cherry twirled her wand around. "Don't worry," she said, "I'll work some magic so that it will seem as if you've only been gone from the party for a moment."

And so, with a blur of bright colours, Kirsty and Rachel found themselves whizzing through the air towards Fairyland.

"Hello," they heard a sweet voice calling as they landed with a bump. "Which one of you is Kirsty and which one is Rachel? I've heard so much about you, my dears."

Kirsty and Rachel blinked and looked around. They were now fairy-sized themselves. And there, standing in front of them, was somebody who could only be the Fairy Godmother. She had long copper hair swept up into a ponytail, the kindest green eyes that Rachel and Kirsty had ever seen, and wings that shimmered every time they moved.

"I'm Kirsty," Kirsty said, jumping up at once.

"And I'm Rachel," Rachel added, scrambling to her feet.

"Delighted to meet you at last," the Fairy Godmother replied, dropping a beautiful curtsey.

Then her eyes narrowed at the sight of the goblin, standing next to Cherry. "I see that you've taken something that doesn't belong to you," she said sternly, pointing a finger at Cherry's party bag.

Whizz! The party bag glowed with red and purple light and shot out of the goblin's hands at once. It zoomed straight over to Cherry, who clutched it with relief.

"Thank you!" she cried.

"You're welcome, my dear," the Fairy Godmother said. Then she fixed her gaze on the goblin. "As for you, I've got just the thing to teach you a lesson." She pointed a finger at him. "You'll need that," she said, "and that."

Kirsty and Rachel couldn't help laughing as an enormous chef's hat suddenly appeared on the goblin's head, and a crisp white apron wrapped itself around his body.

"You can help in the Party Workshop for the rest of the week, icing all the cakes," the Fairy Godmother went on firmly. "Let's hope that keeps you out of mischief."

The goblin looked very sulky as Cherry bustled him away. "You won't catch the other goblins so easily," he snarled. "We'll get the rest of those party bags, just you wait and see!"

Once he'd gone, the Fairy Godmother turned back to Kirsty and Rachel. "I'm afraid he might be right," she told them. "Jack Frost's goblins can be very cunning, as you know. They'll try every trick they can think of to steal the other magical party bags. All you can do is look out for trouble at human parties," she said. "The goblins are likely to try and spoil them because they know that the Party Fairies will rush to help. That will give them the chance they need to steal the fairies' party bags."

"We'll keep a look-out," Rachel promised.

At that moment, Cherry returned. "We'd better send you back to your party," she told the girls. "And don't worry – I'm sure there won't be any more goblins to spoil your fun today." She carefully opened her party bag and reached inside. Then, just as the Fairy Godmother pointed her wand at the girls and called, "Home!" Cherry threw a handful of red and purple fairy dust over them.

The world seemed to spin, there was a sweet, sugary smell in the air and then the girls found themselves back in Kirsty's kitchen.

"Jessica's the winner!" they heard Mrs Tate saying. "Come and get your prize for being the best statue!"

"It sounds like the game's only just finished," Kirsty said happily. "Just like Cherry promised. Let's go and join the party again, Rachel."

But Rachel was staring at the kitchen table in wonder. "Look, Kirsty!" she gulped. "Look at your cake!"

Kirsty gasped in surprise. Yellow and red fairy hundreds and thousands were floating down. The cake melted into thin air, while a new cake formed in its place. Kirsty and Rachel stared in wonder as three tiers appeared, one by one, beautifully covered with pretty pink icing.

Suddenly, they heard Mrs Tate calling for them. "Kirsty! Rachel! Where are you?"

"Time to go," Rachel said.

Very carefully, the girls lifted the magnificent cake. As they carried it into the living room together, the little silver bells tinkled merrily.

"Wow!" cried Kirsty's friend Jessica. "I've never seen anything like it."

Another girl, Molly, was licking her lips. "It's almost too beautiful to eat," she said. "Although it smells so gorgeous, I'll give it a try!"

Mrs Tate looked dazzled. "It's a work of art!" she said to her husband in amazement.

Mr Tate was staring at the cake, too, with a bewildered expression on his face. "Well... Um... It's not so difficult when you know how," he said sheepishly.

"Shall we cut the cake, Mum?" Kirsty interrupted quickly.

"Good idea," Mrs Tate replied. She lit the candles, and everybody sang 'Happy Birthday'.

As they tucked into slices of the delicious birthday cake, they both thought of their new fairy mission with excitement.

"I can't wait to meet the other Party Fairies," Rachel whispered to Kirsty. "But I'm not looking forward to seeing any more goblins."

"I know," Kirsty agreed. "I just hope we can stop them from spoiling the king and queen's party."

Rachel patted her friend's arm comfortingly. "At least Cherry said there'd be no more trouble at your party," she pointed out. "So we can enjoy the rest of your birthday without worrying."

Kirsty nodded. "Yes," she said. Then she grinned. "An invitation to the king and queen's jubilee party, meeting Cherry and a visit to Fairyland – I just knew this was going to be a wonderful birthday," she sighed happily, "and I was right."

Melodie the Music Fairy

"Kirsty, you're a brilliant dancer!" Rachel Walker smiled, clapping her hands as her friend took a bow. It was the next day, and Kirsty had just finished practising the ballet steps she would be performing later that evening.

"It will look even better with the other dancers and the proper costumes," Kirsty replied with a grin. "And wait till you hear the lovely music."

The girls were going to the village hall for the first anniversary of Kirsty's ballet school. "It's going to be a great party," Kirsty went on. "My ballet teacher is decorating the hall and organising some games, and all the parents are bringing food."

"It sounds fun," Rachel agreed. "As long as no goblins turn up!"

"That's true." Kirsty nodded when suddenly, the girls heard Mrs Tate's voice.

"Time to go, girls!" she called.

Kirsty and Rachel hurried downstairs to join Kirsty's mum and dad.

Mr Tate handed over a tin of fairy cakes that he had made and drove them all to the village hall. "The hall looks so different!" Kirsty gasped.

Several rows of chairs had been set up to face the stage, just like in a real theatre. Shiny silver streamers hung from the ceiling, twinkling fairy lights bordered the stage and bunches of brightly-coloured balloons floated above each table of food.

While Mr and Mrs Tate chatted to other parents, Rachel and Kirsty arranged the fairy cakes on a plate. Just then, the ballet teacher, Miss Kelly, joined them. "Kirsty, it's time for you to go and get

ready now," she said. "And you must be Rachel," she added with a smile. "Kirsty said you would be coming."

"Can I help Kirsty and the other girls get ready?" Rachel asked eagerly.

Miss Kelly nodded. "Thank you, Rachel. I could certainly use another pair of hands."

Kirsty led the way to the dressing room, which was behind the stage. While the dancers slipped into their tights and tutus, Rachel helped Miss Kelly apply rosy powder to the girls' cheeks and a dab of pink gloss to their lips. Finally, the dancers put on their ballet shoes, tying the satin ribbons firmly around their ankles.

There was a feeling of excitement in the air as the audience took their seats. Watching from backstage, Rachel breathed a sigh of relief. The decorations, the food and the costumes were perfect. It looked like Jack Frost's goblins hadn't heard about the ballet-school party after all.

Miss Kelly walked onto the stage. "Ladies and gentlemen, I am pleased to present our very first class of ballerinas, who will perform for you tonight in honour of our school's anniversary," she announced.

The audience clapped as Miss Kelly hurried into the wings. Then the curtain rose, and the music began.

With their arms held gracefully over their heads, the dancers ran daintily onto the stage. Rachel watched in delight – the girls looked as beautiful as fairies in their pretty, gauzy tutus.

But then, suddenly, the music changed. It seemed to speed up and the dancers started to have difficulty staying in time. Although they were dancing on bravely, Rachel could see from Kirsty's face that something was wrong.

She watched in dismay as one or two of the girls stumbled, stubbing their toes on the stage as they tried to pirouette more quickly.

The music was still getting faster and faster, and the tune was now just a squeaky jumble of noise.

Rachel glanced across at Miss Kelly. Red in the face, the teacher was frantically pressing the buttons on the CD-player, but it wasn't making any difference. The dancers whirled and spun, quicker and quicker, but it was impossible for them to keep to the beat. Two dancers bumped into each other, and another tripped over her own feet.

"I can't stop the CD-player!" Miss Kelly gasped. "I don't know what's wrong with it."

But Rachel knew. She was sure that this was the work of one of Jack Frost's goblins!

The girls abandoned their performance, and rushed offstage to see what was going on. A couple of the parents came too, to help Miss Kelly with the music. But nobody seemed to know what was wrong with the CD-player.

"This is definitely goblin mischief!" Rachel said to herself. She looked for Kirsty, but couldn't see her in the crowd of people backstage. "Well, I'm going to find him and stop his tricks!"

Rachel glanced round the village hall, and her heart sank. She could see lots of places where a goblin could hide. Backstage there were trunks and racks of costumes and the big cardboard set from

the last pantomime – not to mention two dressing rooms, a music room and a tiny office.

But then, just as Rachel was wondering where to start her search, she saw a pile of musical instruments stacked in the wings on the other side of the stage. And one of them, a tambourine, was shaking, all on its own!

The tambourine was too small to hide a goblin, so what could be making it tremble?

As quietly as she could, Rachel slipped across the stage to the other side. Very carefully, Rachel lifted the rim with one finger.

As she did so, a golden glow flooded out from underneath.

Rachel grinned and lifted the tambourine away eagerly. She had already guessed what she would find, and sure enough, tucked away with her face buried in her gauzy skirt, was a tiny, shimmering fairy.

"You're a Party Fairy!" Rachel exclaimed with delight.

The fairy raised her head. She was sobbing so hard that she had been making the tambourine bells jingle. Tears like tiny diamonds rolled down her cheeks as she adjusted her little gold hairband. "That's r-right, I'm Melodie the Music Fairy," she sniffed sadly. "And you must be Rachel."

Melodie stood up on tiptoe. She was wearing a beautiful pink ballet dress, with black musical notes all around the hem. Her hair was in plaits that swung as she turned her head.

"Where's Kirsty?" Melodie asked.

"She's not far away," Rachel told her. "But why are you crying?"

Melodie wiped away a last sparkling tear. "I came to fix the music," she explained. "If I had known one of those nasty goblins had made it go wrong, I would have been more careful. He grabbed my party bag and ran off with it. Now I can't fix the music for the girls' ballet. And if I don't get my party bag back, there won't be any music for the king and queen's jubilee party, either!"

"Don't worry, Melodie," said Rachel. "Kirsty and I will help you get your party bag back."

Melodie brightened immediately. She picked up her glittering wand and fluttered into the pocket of Rachel's skirt. Then Rachel made her way back towards the people gathered around the CD-player.

Kirsty spotted her friend coming across the stage, and hurried to meet her. "Rachel, I think I know what happened to the music," Kirsty whispered in her ear. "It's goblin trouble!"

Rachel nodded. "Look!" she said, and held her skirt pocket open so Kirsty could peek inside.

Melodie waved at her. "Hello, Kirsty. I'm Melodie the Music Fairy," she called in her soft silvery voice.

"Oh, Melodie, I'm so pleased to see you," Kirsty said gratefully. "If anyone can help us, you can."

"She came here to fix the music," Rachel explained. "But a goblin stole her party bag."

Kirsty's face fell. "Oh, no!" she gasped. "We have to get it back before the goblin escapes and takes it to Jack Frost!"

Melodie nodded enthusiastically.

"But where should we start looking?" she asked.

Rachel thought about this. "There are so many people in the main hall, I don't think he would hang around there," she said. "Let's check the other rooms backstage."

With all the noise and confusion, the girls were able to slip away easily without being noticed. They hurried along the backstage corridor, and ran into the ladies' dressing room. Rachel looked in the lockers where the dancers had left their clothes, while Kirsty checked the cupboards and rummaged through the costumes. But there was no sign of a goblin.

Next, they tried the office. Melodie flew out of Rachel's pocket to look under the desk, Rachel peered out of the window, and Kirsty opened all the drawers in the filing cabinet.

The three returned to the corridor feeling a little downhearted when suddenly Kirsty frowned. "I can hear something!" she exclaimed, listening hard. "Someone's playing the piano."

"But who would practise the piano with a party going on?" asked Rachel

Kirsty listened again. "Well, whoever it is, they certainly need the practice," she said, pulling a face. "It sounds terrible!"

Melodie's face lit up. "Only a goblin could play that badly!" she gasped, and immediately she zoomed off

towards the sound. The girls ran after her. As they got closer to the music room, the jangling sound of the piano grew louder.

They found the door ajar, and peeped cautiously into the room. They could hear the terrible music clearly now, and they could even see the piano standing in the middle of the floor. But to their astonishment, there was nobody playing it!

The girls stared in amazement. Even Melodie looked puzzled. But then Rachel had an idea. "Maybe the goblin's hiding inside the piano!" she said. "And playing it from there."

"I'll go and look," Kirsty replied. "Ballet shoes are soft. If the goblin is in there, he won't hear me coming."

"Good idea," Rachel agreed.

Kirsty slipped through the open door and tiptoed over to the grand piano. Holding her breath, she carefully lifted the lid and peeked inside.

And there he was – a nasty-looking goblin, laughing gleefully

and running up and down the piano strings, with Melodie's party bag swinging from one knobbly hand.

As he pranced, he sang to himself in a croaky voice: "I've got the party bag, I'm such a smarty. I'll take it to Jack Frost, and he'll throw a party!"

Ever so gently, Kirsty lowered the piano lid. Then she turned to the door and nodded at Rachel and Melodie.

Melodie frowned thoughtfully, as Rachel looked around the room. There was a set of drums not far from the grand piano, and on one of the drums lay a pair of cymbals. This gave Rachel a clever idea. "See those cymbals?" she said, pointing them out to Melodie. "Do you think you could lift one?"

"I think so," Melodie replied, looking at Rachel curiously.

"Great! I'll take the other," Rachel said.

"But how will you get there to pick it up?" Melodie asked. "If you walk across the room, the goblin might hear you."

"Not if I'm a fairy…" Rachel smiled.

Melodie nodded and waved her wand. A shower of glittering fairy dust floated down around Rachel and she felt herself shrinking.

By the time the sparkling dust had settled, Rachel was as tiny as Melodie herself. She fluttered her wings happily and flew around in a little circle. Then she set off across the music room, with Melodie close behind.

The cymbals were heavy. Melodie and Rachel both had to struggle to lift them, but at last they managed it.

Quickly, they flew over to Kirsty, who had been watching them in bewilderment. Rachel whispered in Kirsty's ear so the goblin wouldn't hear.

"When I wink, open the lid of the piano," she said.

Kirsty nodded.

Rachel and Melodie held up the cymbals and hovered in the air, face to face. Then Rachel winked at Kirsty who immediately lifted the piano lid. At the very same moment, Rachel and Melodie rushed towards each other. And with a crash that shook the room, the cymbals clashed together right above the goblin's head!

The goblin let out a loud scream, clapped his hands over his ears and dropped Melodie's party bag. "Oh, what a dreadful noise!" he shrieked. "My poor head hurts!" And he leapt out of the piano and ran from the room at top speed.

Rachel smiled to herself. The cymbals had made a deafening noise, she thought, but at least she and Melodie had been ready for it. She heard a smaller crash, and looked round to see that Melodie had dropped her cymbal and swooped into the piano to snatch up her party bag.

"Ooh, that was fun!" Melodie exclaimed. "The goblin escaped, but I've got my party bag and that's all that matters." She opened the bag and peeped inside. As she did so, some glittering, golden musical notes drifted out. "And it's still full of magic fairy dust," she declared happily.

At that moment, Kirsty heard footsteps in the corridor outside. "Quick, you two, hide in the piano!"

Rachel dropped her cymbal with a clatter and flew to join Melodie inside the piano. Kirsty let the lid down quickly.

She was just in time. The door to the room swung open, and Miss Kelly came in. "Hello, Kirsty, are you all right?" she asked anxiously. "Whatever was all that noise?"

"Er, I thought that there, um, might be another CD-player in this room," Kirsty explained. "I was looking for it when I knocked over the cymbals."

Miss Kelly laughed. "Well, we need you on stage now. I think we'll be able to start the ballet again in a minute. Melissa's dad is an electrician, and he's fixing the CD-player."

Kirsty frowned. Could a human electrician fix a machine that was broken by a goblin? She had a feeling that only fairy magic would get that CD-player working again. And she knew just who could help. But Melodie was stuck inside the piano with Rachel!

"I'll come in a moment, Miss Kelly," Kirsty said, thinking fast. "Some sequins fell off my costume. I just need to find them first."

"Your costume looks fine," the ballet teacher told her briskly. "A sequin or two makes no difference. We don't want to keep our audience waiting any longer."

Kirsty had no choice. Reluctantly, she followed Miss Kelly out of the music room, leaving Rachel and Melodie trapped inside the piano.

"Oh, no!" Rachel cried after Kirsty and Miss Kelly had gone. "Who knows how long we're going to be stuck in here now?"

Melodie laughed, a tinkling musical sound. "Don't worry, Rachel," she said. And with a wave of her magic wand, the piano lid flew open in a shower of sparkling fairy magic.

Rachel and Melodie flew out. As soon as Rachel reached the ground, Melodie waved her wand again and turned Rachel back to her normal size. Then, clutching her party bag, Melodie hid herself in Rachel's pocket. "We can save the party now," she said happily. "Let's go!"

As Rachel hurried out of the music room, she noticed that the squeaky, speeded-up music had stopped. She wondered if the spell had been broken when the goblin ran away. Or maybe Melissa's dad had fixed the CD-player somehow.

When she reached the stage, however, she saw a large group of people still gathered around the machine. Peering through the crowd, Rachel caught a glimpse of Melissa's dad with a screwdriver in one hand and a pair of pliers in the other.

"I'm terribly sorry," he was saying to Miss Kelly. "I've repaired CD-players before, but I've never seen anything like this. I don't think I can fix it."

"Do you think you can fix it?" Rachel whispered to Melodie.

"Yes, I'm sure I can – with fairy magic," Melodie answered. She peeped out of Rachel's pocket and her face fell. "But not with all these people around," she added. "Someone would see me sprinkling fairy dust over the machine."

"Maybe I can get everyone to move away," Rachel said thoughtfully. But though she racked her brains, she couldn't think of anything that would make the people leave the CD-player.

She looked round quickly, and then she remembered the musical instruments in the wings on the other side of the stage, where she had first found Melodie.

Gently, she lifted the little fairy out of her pocket. "Look," she said softly. "I've got an idea. Can you do anything with those musical instruments instead?"

Melodie smiled and clapped her hands. "Yes, I can!" she exclaimed. "Is anyone looking?"

"No, we're out of sight round here," Rachel told her.

Quickly, Melodie fluttered over to the instruments and perched lightly on the violin. She took a handful of glittering musical notes from her party bag, and carefully sprinkled them over the violin's strings.

Then she flitted from instrument to instrument, throwing a few sparkling notes over each one. Finally, she waved her wand with an expert flourish.

At once, the bow that had been lying next to the violin floated into the air and began stroking the violin's strings.

The flute hovered, quivering, as soft, sweet sounds poured from it, while the strings of a harp were plucked by invisible fingers. Rachel heard the deep, low notes of a horn and watched in amazement as all the instruments began to play themselves.

From across the stage, Rachel heard Miss Kelly exclaim in surprise. "That's our ballet music!" she cried. "Where is it coming from?"

Rachel ran back to the group. "I found another CD-player," she told the ballet teacher. She caught Kirsty's eye and smiled. Rachel didn't have to tell her friend that there was fairy magic at work!

"Quickly, dancers take your places," Miss Kelly called. As the girls rushed onto the stage, the audience moved back to their seats.

Miss Kelly turned to Rachel. "Could you start the music from the beginning again, please?" she asked.

Anxiously, Rachel hurried back to Melodie and the instruments. "Can you do it again?" Rachel asked her.

Melodie's wand fluttered and she threw a few more glittering musical notes into the air. The music stopped for an instant, and then began.

As Kirsty and the others began to dance, Rachel and Melodie watched the performance from the wings.

"Oh, it's lovely!" Melodie exclaimed, copying the dancers' graceful arm movements.

"Just like it should be," Rachel agreed.

The ballet went perfectly, and at the end the audience applauded wildly. The girls curtseyed, left the stage and went to join their proud parents. Except for Kirsty, who rushed over to the side of the stage.

"Thank you, Melodie," she said gratefully. "You saved our party."

"No, thank you," Melodie beamed. "Without you, there would be no music at the king and queen's jubilee. Please keep an eye out for any more of Jack Frost's goblins."

"We will," Rachel and Kirsty promised together.

Melodie beamed. "Good luck," she said, and with a wave of her wand and a shower of twinkling lights, the fairy flew away.

Smiling happily, Rachel and Kirsty made their way to the hall to enjoy the rest of the party.

"I hope we meet more Party Fairies," Rachel said.

"Oh, I'm sure we will," replied Kirsty, and then she smiled. "As long as we keep going to parties!" she added.

Grace
the Glitter
Fairy

Chapter Three

Grace the Glitter Fairy

"Isn't it a beautiful day?" Kirsty Tate said happily, looking up at the deep blue sky.

It was a couple of days later, and Kirsty was sitting on the grass in the Tates' back garden, making a daisy chain with Rachel. Pearl was snoozing in a patch of sunshine in the middle of the path. Suddenly, there was a scrabbling noise behind the hedge.

"OW!" someone muttered. "That hurt."

And at that moment, Mr Cooper, the next-door neighbour, popped his head over the hedge. He was a tall, thin man with a cheerful smile. "Sorry, Kirsty," he said, "did I startle you? I pricked my finger on the rosebush. I'm trying to hide these presents around the garden for the treasure hunt this afternoon." He held up a small parcel wrapped in shiny blue paper.

"Treasure hunt?" repeated Rachel, looking puzzled.

Mr Cooper nodded. "Yes, it's my son Jamie's birthday today,"

he replied. "He's five and we're having a party."

A party! Rachel and Kirsty glanced at each other in excitement.

"We've got ten children coming," Mr Cooper went on. "And we've hired a clown called Mr Chuckles. Jamie is really excited." He smiled and shook his head. "It's going to be a lot of hard work, though."

Rachel nudged Kirsty, who knew exactly what her friend was thinking.

"Maybe Rachel and I could come over and give you and Mrs Cooper a hand?" Kirsty suggested.

"We'd love to," Rachel added eagerly.

Mr Cooper's face lit up. "That's very kind of you," he beamed. "Jamie would love that. The guests are arriving at three o'clock, so could you come at two?"

"Of course we will," Rachel and Kirsty said together.

Mr Cooper gave them a grateful smile, and went off to hide some more parcels.

Kirsty turned to Rachel, her eyes wide with excitement. "Do you think a goblin will turn up and try to spoil Jamie's party?" she asked.

"I don't know," Rachel replied. "But if one does, we'll be ready for him!"

"This is going to be fun," Kirsty grinned, as she rang the Coopers' doorbell. "Jamie is really sweet. It'll be a bit noisy, though, with him and all his friends running around enjoying themselves."

"Maybe they'll frighten any goblins away!" Rachel said with a laugh.

The front door opened. A small boy with exactly the same cheerful smile as Mr Cooper stood in the hallway.

"Hello, Kirsty," Jamie called eagerly. "Are you and your friend here to help with my party?"

"Yes, we are," Kirsty replied, smiling and handing Jamie a parcel. "Happy birthday."

Jamie tore off the wrapping paper excitedly and beamed when he saw the bright red car inside. "Thank you! Come on," he said, taking Kirsty's hand. "Me and Mummy are putting up decorations in the lounge."

Rachel and Kirsty followed him down the hallway. Mrs Cooper was standing on a chair, pinning a HAPPY BIRTHDAY banner to the wall.

"Hello, Kirsty," she smiled. "And it's Rachel, isn't it? It's so kind of you to help out. Thank you."

"Mum!" Jamie was dancing around the lounge, waving his new car. "Look what Kirsty and Rachel gave me! And can we put up the streamers now? Can we?"

"There's still an hour to go and he's already fizzing with excitement," Mrs Cooper said, laughing. "Would you girls be able to put up the streamers and balloons, while I go and help finish off the food?"

"Of course we can," Rachel replied.

Mrs Cooper thanked the girls and hurried off to the kitchen.

Jamie grabbed the box of decorations from the sofa. "Daddy bought some new extra-long streamers," said Jamie proudly. "They're multicoloured – look!"

He began unrolling one of the streamers. But before he had got very far, a piece about fifty centimetres long dropped off and floated to the ground.

"Oh!" Jamie gasped.

"I'm sure the rest of it is OK," Rachel said quickly. "Keep going, Jamie."

But as Jamie unrolled the streamer, more lengths of brightly-coloured paper fell off. Rachel opened the other packets, but those streamers had been spoiled in exactly the same way.

"It's just as if someone has cut the streamers and then rolled them back up again," Kirsty whispered to Rachel.

Rachel nodded solemnly. "Do you think it could be goblin mischief?" she asked.

Jamie was looking close to tears. "They're too short!" he wailed.

"Don't worry, Jamie," Kirsty said, giving him a hug. "I've got just the thing to fix this. I won't be long."

Kirsty ran home and found a big roll of sparkly, blue sticky-tape, which was left over from Christmas. Then she went back to the Coopers' house and showed it to Jamie.

"Look," she said, beginning to stick the pieces of one of the streamers together. "Now you'll have stripy gold, silver and blue streamers."

Jamie's face lit up. "They look even better now!" he declared happily.

The three of them quickly stuck the rest of the streamers together and then Rachel and Kirsty began to pin them up around the room. They had just finished when there was a ring at the doorbell.

"That'll be Mr Chuckles," Mrs Cooper called from the kitchen. "Could you let him in, please, Kirsty?"

"I think Jamie has beaten me to it," Kirsty chuckled, as Jamie dashed past her into the hall.

Rachel and Kirsty followed him, and found the clown standing on the doorstep, smiling down at Jamie. He wore a bright purple, baggy suit and a green bowler hat.

"You must be the birthday boy," he said.

Looking as if he was about to burst with excitement, Jamie ran to tell his mum about the clown.

Meanwhile, Mr Chuckles turned to Rachel and Kirsty. "Is it OK if I set up my stuff in the lounge?" he asked.

Kirsty nodded. "Yes, we've almost finished decorating," she replied. "We've just got the balloons to blow up."

The clown opened the back of his van and began to unload his props, while the girls went back into the lounge. But to their dismay, the streamers which they had so carefully pinned up earlier had all fallen down. Now they lay in heaps on the floor.

"Quick, let's get these back up or Jamie will be upset," Kirsty said, picking up the sticky-tape.

The girls worked fast and got the streamers back in place before Jamie came bouncing into the room.

"We're going to blow up the balloons now, Jamie," said Kirsty, opening one of the packets. "Which colour shall we start with?"

"Gold!" Jamie called eagerly.

Kirsty began to blow air into the long gold balloon. But although she huffed and puffed and got red in the face, the balloon wouldn't inflate. It remained as flat as a pancake.

"There's a hole in it," Rachel said, peering closely at the balloon.

The girls exchanged a look. They were both thinking exactly the same thing. A goblin had definitely been at work.

Quickly, she and Rachel checked all the other balloons. There were holes in all of them! Jamie's bottom lip was trembling.

"Are all the balloons spoiled?" he asked in a small voice.

At that moment, Mr Chuckles came into the lounge carrying a large wooden box. "Is it balloons you need?" he asked. "I've got some spares." He put his hand into

his pocket and pulled out a handful of different-coloured balloons. "I use them to make my balloon animals."

Kirsty and Rachel were very relieved to see Jamie smiling again. Quickly, they blew up the balloons and hung them around the French windows at the far end of the room.

Suddenly, the doorbell rang. Jamie peeped out of the front window. "It's Matthew, my best friend!" he shouted excitedly. "And Katie and Andy and Ben. It's time for my party to start!" And he dashed out to meet his guests.

"Goodness me, I must go to the bathroom and put my clown make-up on," said Mr Chuckles. He grabbed a small case and left the room.

POP! POP! POP! Kirsty and Rachel jumped and turned round. The balloons they had just put up were bursting, one by one.

"I'm starting to get very fed up with that goblin," Rachel said crossly.

"So am I," Kirsty agreed. "We need to find him and put a stop to his tricks!"

The doorbell was ringing again as more guests arrived, and the girls could hear them chattering excitedly in the hall.

Then they heard Mr Cooper's voice. "Follow me out to the garden, kids," he was saying. "We're going to have a treasure hunt!"

There was a loud cheer as the children hurried after him, and Rachel and Kirsty looked at each other in relief.

"Let's search the room," Kirsty suggested. "We might be able to deal with the goblin while everyone's in the garden."

But just as they began their search, Rachel pointed towards the French windows. "Look – outside in the garden."

Kirsty peered through the glass to see a sparkling pink shape flying swiftly through the air. It was zooming straight through the garden, towards the French windows of the lounge.

"It's Grace the Glitter Fairy!" Kirsty gasped.

"Yes," said Rachel anxiously. "And the children are going out into the garden. They'll all see her unless we do something – and fast!"

"We have to go outside and warn her," Kirsty said.

"What about the goblin?" Rachel asked.

"This is more important," Kirsty replied, opening the French windows.

She and Rachel rushed outside, waving their arms madly to get Grace's attention.

Grace saw them straightaway and waved her sparkling pink wand at them. She had long, straight, glossy blonde hair, and she wore a glittering rose-coloured dress, which shimmered in the sunshine. The hem of the dress was red and cut into handkerchief points. The floaty skirt swirled around her legs as she hovered in mid-air.

"Hello, girls," she called, "It's good to see you—"

"Grace, you have to hide!" Kirsty burst out, without even saying hello. "The party guests are about to come out into the garden any minute!"

But, before Grace could say anything, they heard the back door open.

"So that's what you have to do, kids," Mr Cooper was saying. "Off you go."

Grace looked alarmed as all the children came galloping out of the back door. "Thanks for warning me, girls," she gasped. And she fluttered out of sight behind a garden urn filled with flowers.

The children were running all round the garden now, screaming with excitement. Two little girls came over to where Kirsty and Rachel were standing, and began to search for presents there.

"Er, I think Mr Cooper hid most of the presents at the bottom of the garden," Rachel said quickly. The girls ran off straightaway.

Kirsty and Rachel sighed with relief as Grace appeared from behind the garden urn. "Thank you for saving me!" she said.

"There's a goblin here," Rachel told Grace, as the little fairy smoothed down her hair. "He's been ruining all the party decorations in the lounge."

"Well, we'll soon put a stop to that!" Grace declared, looking outraged. "Where is he?"

"We don't know," Kirsty replied. "We were just about to start looking for him, when we saw you coming."

Grace nodded. "Well, now I can help you find him," she said, smiling. "Lead the way!"

As Kirsty led the way through the French windows into the lounge, she suddenly gasped and caught Rachel's arm. "Look, there!" she breathed. "Behind the curtain."

Rachel and Grace looked
at the long blue curtains
hanging either side of
the French windows,
and immediately saw
what Kirsty had spotted
– behind one of them,
there was a definite
goblin-shape!

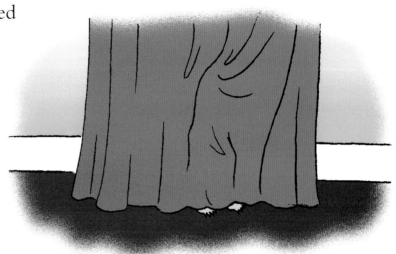

They all stared at the goblin
bulge behind the curtain. They saw it shift once or twice. The goblin
was obviously getting a bit fed up.

Kirsty beckoned Rachel and Grace to follow her to the other
end of the room. "We need to do something right now," Kirsty
whispered. "Before Jamie
and his friends come in
from the garden."

"Yes, but what?"
Grace queried, biting
her lip anxiously.

"We could creep up
on the goblin and grab him
while he's wrapped in the
curtain," Rachel suggested.
"It shouldn't be too difficult. He's quite small."

She and Rachel crept cautiously towards the French windows,
with Grace fluttering alongside. They had nearly reached the goblin,

when the lounge door suddenly opened and Mrs Cooper appeared, laden with plates of food. Quick as a flash, Grace darted into Kirsty's pocket, out of sight.

"Ah, girls," said Jamie's mum. "Could you possibly give me a hand with these snacks?"

Rachel and Kirsty exchanged an agonised look, but there was nothing they could do.

"Yes, of course," Kirsty replied politely, and the girls hurried to help Mrs Cooper set the plates down on the dining table.

"As soon as the children have finished the treasure hunt, we'll bring them in here," Mrs Cooper told the girls. "They can have a snack before they watch Mr Chuckles, and then after his show, we'll have tea."

The girls nodded and Mrs Cooper headed back to the kitchen.

As soon as she had gone, Grace fluttered out of Kirsty's pocket and the girls turned back to tackle the goblin. But it was too late!

"Oh, no!" gasped Rachel, as she looked around the room. The goblin-shape behind the curtain had vanished!

At that very moment, the three friends heard a scrabbling noise behind the sofa.

"The goblin must be hiding over there!" Rachel whispered excitedly, pointing to the sofa.

Kirsty's face lit up. "How about we use Grace's party bag as bait to catch the goblin. We can wrap him up in the tablecloth instead of the curtain, and then Grace can still whisk him off to Fairyland!"

"Good idea," Grace whispered. "We'll hide behind that armchair, and catch him red-handed." Then she spoke again in a louder voice. "My party bag's so heavy, girls," she said with a wink. "It's because I've got so much magic fairy dust in it."

"Why don't you put it down on the coffee table?" Rachel suggested, glancing at the sofa.

"Then you can come into the kitchen with us, and we'll show you Jamie's beautiful birthday cake," added Kirsty, picking up a shiny, cream-coloured tablecloth. "It's in the shape of a steam train."

"OK," Grace agreed. She pulled her multicoloured party bag from her pocket, and placed it carefully on the coffee table. "Let's go then."

But instead of leaving the room, they all tiptoed over to the armchair, and hid behind it. It was a bit of a squash. Kirsty and Rachel were too big to both fit behind the chair.

"Wait a moment," Grace whispered.

She twirled her wand in the air and there was a sparkle of fairy dust. In a second, Rachel and Kirsty had shrunk to fairy-size, with glittering wings on their backs. Kirsty fluttered her wings happily. Grace looked pleased. "That's better,"

she said, glancing at the sofa. "And we're just in time. Here he comes…"

The goblin poked his head round the edge of the sofa to see if the coast was clear. Then he stepped out. His beady little eyes gleamed as he saw the party bag lying on the coffee table, and he hurried to pick it up.

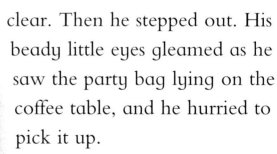

But as he reached for the party bag, Grace, Kirsty and Rachel zoomed out of their hiding place, each holding a corner of the tablecloth.

"Get him!" Rachel yelled.

They hovered above the surprised goblin, and dropped the tablecloth right over him. He gave a shout of fury as it covered him completely from head to toe.

"It worked!" cried Kirsty. But the goblin began to rip the tablecloth to shreds!

"He's tearing his way out!" Kirsty exclaimed. "What shall we do?"

Rachel looked round, spotted the streamers on the floor and had an idea. She grabbed the end of one of them, and flew swiftly round and round the goblin, tying him up.

"Quick, Kirsty!" Grace called, as she saw what Rachel was doing. "Grab a streamer."

"Stop it!" the goblin called crossly. He tried to fight his way out, but Grace and the girls were wrapping him up too quickly. A few minutes later he couldn't move. He looked just like an Egyptian mummy.

"Ohhh!" the goblin groaned sulkily.

"Serves you right," Rachel told him, as Grace rescued her precious party bag.

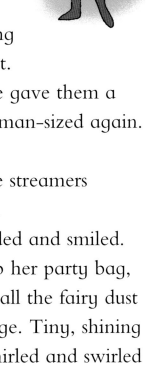

Meanwhile, Kirsty had fluttered over to the French windows to check on the treasure hunt.

"OK, kids, you've found all the presents," Mr Cooper was saying. "Now it's time to see Mr Chuckles, the clown."

"Jamie and his friends are coming in now, Grace," Kirsty called. "You'd better go."

Grace turned to the goblin. "And you're coming with me," she laughed.

She waved her wand, and the moaning, grumbling goblin disappeared in a cloud of sparkling fairy dust.

"Goodbye, girls, and thank you," Grace said. She gave them a hug, and with a wave of her wand, made them human-sized again.

Then Kirsty remembered the decorations.

"Grace, can you help?" she asked, pointing at the streamers and balloons.

Grace nodded and smiled. She tipped up her party bag, and emptied all the fairy dust into the lounge. Tiny, shining diamonds whirled and swirled around the room, spinning into every corner.

When the magic dust had cleared, Kirsty and Rachel were delighted to see that the walls were festooned with

glittering, rainbow-coloured streamers and balloons. There was even a new paper tablecloth, and when Kirsty and Rachel spread it out on the table, they saw that it was shinier than before and covered with a sprinkling of gleaming gold stars.

"Thank you!" the girls cried in amazement.

Grace gave a silvery laugh, waved her wand and disappeared, just as the children charged in led by Mr Cooper. They all stopped and stared in amazement at the fabulous decorations.

"Wow!" Jamie gasped. "Look what Kirsty and Rachel have done, Dad!"

"It's fantastic, girls," said Mr Cooper gratefully.

Rachel and Kirsty beamed at each other, and sat down with the party guests to watch Mr Chuckles perform. The clown was very funny and had everyone in fits of laughter with a giant, water-squirting sunflower. Rachel and Kirsty enjoyed it just as much as Jamie and his friends.

At the end of the show, Mr Chuckles told them he was going to make some balloon animals. When he opened his bag and pulled out a handful of balloons, there was a gasp of wonder.

They were the most wonderful, colourful balloons anyone had ever seen – and some were even striped and spotted with animal-print designs.

Mr Chuckles stared at them in delight. "I didn't even know I had these," he muttered.

Rachel and Kirsty smiled. They knew where those balloons had come from – Grace the Glitter Fairy!

Mr Chuckles began to twist and tie the balloons together. He made an elephant first, which he gave to Jamie. Then he made a lovely giraffe and a zebra.

"These are for the two girls who put up these beautiful decorations," Mr Chuckles said. He bowed, and presented the giraffe to Rachel and the zebra to Kirsty. The girls were thrilled.

And so was somebody else…

"This is my best birthday ever!" Jamie beamed, as the clown began to make animals for all the other children.

"And we've saved another Party Fairy and her party bag," Rachel whispered happily to Kirsty. "Hurray!"

Honey
the Sweet
Fairy

Chapter Four

Honey the Sweet Fairy

It was a lovely, sunny day, and Mr and Mrs Tate had set lunch outside in the garden. As Kirsty and Rachel sat down to eat, Mrs Tate suddenly groaned aloud.

"I knew there was something else I meant to get from the shops this morning," she cried. "Gran's toffees! I promised I'd take her some this evening, and I completely forgot to buy them."

Kirsty put down her sandwich. "Don't worry, Mum. We'll go to Mrs Twist's Sweet Shop after lunch for you," she suggested. She glanced at Rachel. The two girls smiled at each other.

"That reminds me," Mr Tate said. "I saw in the local newspaper that Mrs Twist is retiring. Her daughter's taking over the sweet shop from tomorrow. As this is her last day, Mrs Twist is throwing a party for all her customers." He winked at

Kirsty and Rachel. "I read something about there being plenty of free sweets up for grabs, too!"

Kirsty nudged Rachel at once. "Sweets and a party," she repeated. "How exciting! But you know we really do need to check it out – just in case another goblin turns up to cause trouble."

Rachel nodded. "Our work isn't over yet!"

After lunch, Mrs Tate gave the girls some money for the toffees, and they set out for the sweet shop.

As they turned into the High Street, they saw some other children clustered outside Mrs Twist's shop. But as they drew nearer, Kirsty and Rachel realised that something was wrong.

A boy was pulling a face as he licked a lollipop. And one little girl started to cry. "These sweeties taste funny," she wailed.

Kirsty and Rachel went into the shop, wondering what was going on.

The tiny shop looked very festive. Colourful balloons hung from the ceiling, and party streamers were twined around the big jars of sweets

that lined the shelves. Mrs Twist stood behind the counter as usual – but Kirsty noticed at once that she didn't look her normal cheerful self.

"Hello, Mrs Twist," Kirsty called. "Is everything all right?"

Mrs Twist shook her head sadly. "Not really," she replied. "It's my last day and I was hoping to have a wonderful party, but all my sweets are spoiled!"

As Kirsty and Rachel looked around, they could see what Mrs Twist meant. The pineapple chunks that she was trying to shake from their jar had become one big, sticky lump. The chocolate bars were soft and soggy, as if they'd been lying in the sun. And the sherbet was fizzing so fiercely it made everyone sneeze!

Rachel nudged Kirsty. "Look!" she said in a low voice, pointing at one of the shelves.

Kirsty looked and saw a box of pink sugar mice, all with their paws over their eyes as if they were scared of something. The jelly

babies looked worried too – they were all holding hands. And, to Kirsty's surprise, a group of jelly snakes in a jar were wriggling crossly and actually hissing!

"Something very weird is going on," Rachel whispered. "It's got to be goblin mischief!" she whispered back.

Mrs Twist put down the jar of pineapple cubes, and pulled out a tray of chocolates instead. Then she sighed in dismay. "Oh, no! What's happened to these?"

Rachel and Kirsty went over to look. The sweets had all melted on the tray, and right in the middle was a big hollow where what looked like a goblin footprint had pressed into the soft chocolate!

The girls exchanged glances and Kirsty promptly peered down at the floor. "Look, goblin footprints," she muttered to Rachel.

The girls quietly slipped away from the shop counter to follow the trail of chocolatey footprints. They led to the door to Mrs

Twist's stockroom. Rachel bit her lip when…

CRASH! Both girls jumped as they heard a loud noise from the other side of the door.

"Oh, no! It sounds like the goblin's wreaking havoc in there," Rachel hissed.

Before Kirsty could reply, she heard Mrs Twist saying, "This is no good. I can't give people these spoiled sweets. I'll get some new ones from the stockroom."

"No!" cried Kirsty hurriedly. She couldn't let Mrs Twist go in there – not with a sneaky goblin on the loose!

"I mean, er…" she faltered, as Mrs Twist looked at her in suprise. "You can't leave the shop, Mrs Twist. Rachel and I will fetch the sweets for you."

Mrs Twist smiled. "Thank you, dear," she said gratefully. "Bring out anything you like the look of."

Kirsty nodded and cautiously pushed open the stockroom door. As both girls peeped into the room, they gasped in horror. Bottles and jars had been knocked over, and there were sweets scattered all across the floor. But, worst of all, there was a tiny fairy struggling desperately to hang on to her magical party bag, as a grinning goblin fought to tug it out of her hands!

"It's Honey, the Sweet Fairy!" cried Kirsty. "And she's in trouble!"

Kirsty and Rachel slipped inside the stockroom at once and shut the door behind them.

Honey was wearing a pale yellow dress and little sherbet-yellow shoes. Her golden-brown ponytail swung madly to and fro as she tried to save her party bag. "Oh, girls, please help me!" she cried as she saw the friends.

"We certainly will," Rachel called back fiercely. Her gaze fell on a large jar of sweets. "Gobstoppers!" she exclaimed happily, unscrewing the lid. "Over here, Kirsty."

Both girls took handfuls of the gobstoppers and began pelting the goblin with the hard, round sweets.

"Ouch!" yelped the goblin, as a gobstopper bounced off his long nose. He threw up his arms to protect his face – and let go of the party bag. But he released it so suddenly that Honey shot backwards into one of the shelves. All the breath was knocked out of her and she dropped her precious party bag!

The girls and Honey rushed to scoop up the tiny, sweet-shaped sparkles – but the goblin was already there, grabbing great glittering handfuls.

"Just what Jack Frost wanted," he gloated, stuffing it into his pockets. "Now I've got this fairy dust, his party will be better than ever!"

"Oh, no, it won't!" Kirsty shouted, grabbing a striped candy cane from the floor. Rachel did the same, and the two girls started poking the goblin in the ribs with them.

"Ooh! Ah! Tee hee…" the goblin giggled helplessly, as the canes tickled him. "Stop! Stop it!"

The goblin was laughing so hard that he

lost his balance. He stumbled and skidded on the gobstoppers that were all over the floor. "Whoaaaa!" he cried, his arms flailing. And then, "OW!" he shouted, as he fell over.

All of the fairy dust bounced out of his pockets as he landed and began vanishing before his eyes. The goblin stretched out a gnarly green hand to grab it again, but Honey was too quick for him. She waved her wand at the candy canes and muttered some magical words.

Kirsty and Rachel watched in delight as all the candy canes on the floor started to shimmer with a golden glow. Then they leapt up and marched smartly over to the goblin.

Before he could get his hands on any of the vanishing fairy dust, the stripy canes began herding him across the room and out of the back of the shop.

"That's got rid of him," Rachel laughed, as the door swung shut behind the goblin.

"Phew," Honey sighed with relief, smiling at the girls. Then she fluttered down to look at her party bag, and the smile slipped from her face. "Oh, dear!" she cried.

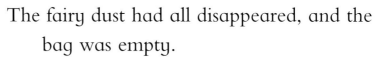

The fairy dust had all disappeared, and the bag was empty.

Kirsty glanced around the stockroom. It was a terrible mess.

"We'd better tidy this up before Mrs Twist sees it," she said anxiously. "It's going to take us ages."

"If only I had some fairy dust, I could magic everything to rights," Honey cried. "But that horrible goblin made me spill it all."

"Girls!" came Mrs Twist's voice from the shop. "Is everything all right in there?"

"Er, yes! We're just coming," Kirsty called back quickly. The girls looked at each other in panic. They could hear the shop bell jingling as yet more customers came in for sweets. What were they going to do?

Honey thought fast. "We'll have to go to Fairyland to the Party Workshop and get new sweets," she said. "I've made heaps for the jubilee party – you can have some of those. And I can refill my party bag with fairy dust, too."

"Brilliant!" Kirsty smiled. "What are we waiting for?"

Honey waved her wand over the girls, and amber sparkles swirled around them. There was a wonderful smell of spun sugar, and the girls felt themselves shrinking. The next thing they knew, they were whizzing through the air very fast.

"Here we are," came Honey's silvery voice a moment later. "Fairyland!"

Kirsty and Rachel blinked and looked round. They were the same size as Honey now – and best of all, they each had a pair of glittering fairy wings. Rachel beamed in delight and gave her wings a quick flutter.

Meanwhile, Kirsty was gazing at the magnificent golden castle that stood before them. Balloons and streamers fluttered from its towers, and jolly music floated from it on the breeze. There was the most delicious smell of baking in the air, too.

"Wow!" exclaimed Rachel. "Who lives here?"

"Nobody lives here," Honey giggled. "This is our Party Workshop."

Kirsty's eyes widened. "Bertram showed us some of the inside, but I never realised the outside looked so lovely," she said.

Honey pushed open a golden gate. "This way," she called.

The girls followed her into the castle.

"This is Cherry's bakery," Honey told them, as they walked through a large, sunny kitchen.

Kirsty licked her lips. There were trays and trays of scrumptious chocolate cakes, strawberry tarts, cream sponges, blueberry muffins and lots more. Some fairies were carefully mixing ingredients, while others were icing the cakes with intricate jubilee designs.

"Look!" Rachel gasped suddenly. "There's the goblin who spoiled your birthday cake, Kirsty. I'd forgotten the Fairy Godmother had sent him here!"

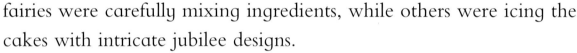
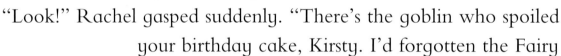

The girls watched as the goblin carefully piped pretty icing flowers onto a cake.

"And to think he spent all that time spoiling cakes," Kirsty whispered to Rachel, "when actually, he's quite good at making them look beautiful!"

Then Honey led the girls through to another huge room, filled with brightly-coloured balloons. There were twinkling fairy lights strung all over the high, arched ceiling, and shining silver streamers twirling in mid-air. But best of all was the fountain of glitter in the middle of the room, which sparkled in all the colours of the rainbow. Grace the Glitter Fairy fluttered about, organising her helpers.

As soon as she saw the girls, she winked and waved her wand at them, sending a swirl of pink glitter shooting towards them in a heart shape.

Rachel and Kirsty smiled and waved and then followed Honey through another door. They found themselves on a golden balcony, overlooking a magnificent hallway.

"We saw this bit when Bertram came to see us," Kirsty remembered. "Look, there's Melodie the Music Fairy – and the frog orchestra!"

It was wonderful to see so many frogs smartly dressed in red waistcoats and playing their musical instruments.

"There's Bertram," Rachel whispered, giving him a wave.

Bertram was so excited to see the girls that he tooted his bugle in all the wrong places.

Kirsty suddenly noticed that there was somebody else in the great hall too – the Fairy Godmother. The girls held their breath as she flew over to greet them.

"Hello again, girls," she smiled. "Have you and Honey been having goblin trouble, by any chance?"

"You could say that," Honey agreed, and she told the Fairy Godmother what had happened in Mrs Twist's sweet shop. The Fairy Godmother chuckled. "Those wretched goblins!" she said. "Well, you'd better take Mrs Twist some magical sweets for her shop. That will make her customers happy again."

"Thank you," Kirsty breathed, her eyes shining.

The Fairy Godmother's eyes twinkled as she looked at the girls' happy faces. Then she lifted her wand and waved it over their heads. "Fly, fairies, fly!" she said. "And keep up the good work."

Rachel was just about to reply when she felt herself swept up in a warm, magical breeze. It lifted both girls off the ground and whisked them along through the air. The Fairy Godmother waved as they drifted away.

Honey laughed. She, too, was caught up in the gale. "It's a magical wind," she cried in delight. "A special fairy breeze that will take us to the Sweet Factory!"

The breeze whisked them along the balcony and into another room, where the girls saw Jasmine the Present Fairy. She was wrapping up gifts in sparkling paper, with long, looping ribbons that tied themselves in perfect bows.

In the next room, Phoebe the Fashion Fairy was hard at work, surrounded by rolls of glittering material, boxes of shiny sequins and rows of sparkling buttons that kept changing shape. There were racks of gowns and outfits in every colour imaginable.

"This is the most exciting place in the world!" Kirsty declared. And then she gasped, and jumped in surprise, as the breeze carried them into a very busy room.

Fairies were dashing all over the place, trying to catch a shiny silver parcel with small pink wings that was zooming from ceiling to floor.

"This is Polly the Party Fun Fairy's room," Honey told the girls, as Polly flew over, smiling.

"This is my new game – Pass the Magic Parcel," Polly explained.

"What fun!" Rachel laughed.

"Bye, Polly," Honey called, catching Kirsty and Rachel's hands and pulling them towards a pair of bright red doors.

"It's my department next – the Sweet Factory," she announced proudly.

The breeze carried the girls and Honey through the doors and out into a sunlit courtyard. Then, just as suddenly as it had appeared, the magical wind died away, and the girls were set gently down on the ground again.

Honey immediately led them along a path to a small orchard. Kirsty and Rachel stared in wonder – the trees seemed to be sparkling!

"Sugar frosting," Honey told them with a grin. She broke off a handful of glittering green leaves. "Here, try these."

Kirsty and Rachel bit into the sugared leaves, which tasted deliciously of lime juice.

"Yummy!" Rachel declared, licking her lips.

"There are pear drops growing on these trees," Honey said, pointing. "And sherbet lemons over there." They all watched as a couple of fairies flew close to the trees, picking the sweets and putting them in golden baskets.

Further along, Rachel spotted some other fairies using great lengths of liquorice as skipping ropes. "What are they doing?" Rachel asked.

"Strength testing," Honey told her. "And making sure it's stretchy enough." She smiled.

Honey filled up her party bag with golden fairy dust from a frothing sherbet fountain, then she took the girls to her own stockroom. It was piled high with boxes and jars of fairy sweets. "Let's see… Fizzy Fairies, Strawberry Sparkles, Peppermint Pops, Chocolate Bubbles…" Honey murmured, loading boxes into the girls' arms.

"May we have some toffees too, please?" Kirsty asked, suddenly remembering the errand her mum had sent her on. It seemed a long time ago now.

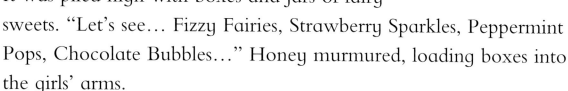

"Of course!" Honey smiled. She waved her wand, and a jar of toffees appeared at the top of Kirsty's pile.

"Fantastic," Rachel beamed. "Now Mrs Twist is going to have a wonderful leaving party!"

"It's time for me to take you home," Honey said, once the girls were fully laden. She waved her wand again and Rachel and Kirsty found themselves surrounded by amber sparkles. Fairyland seemed to melt away before their eyes, there was a delicious smell of honey, a whirl of colours and then…

"Girls? Have you found the sweets?" Mrs Twist was calling.

No time had passed at all. Honey, Rachel and Kirsty were back in the stockroom of the sweet shop and back to their normal size, too.

"Coming!" Kirsty called breathlessly.

"I'll just sort this mess out before I go," Honey said, and she drew a handful of fairy dust from her party bag and threw it into the air. For a moment, the whole stockroom glowed with golden light – and then the fun began! The jelly snakes started wiggling their way back to their jar. The gobstoppers bounced into a jar and whizzed around inside it with a noisy rattle, and the jelly babies hopped into their box one by one.

As soon as all the jars and boxes were full, they flew back onto their shelves and lined themselves up neatly.

Honey gave a little curtsey in mid-air, then flew over to hug both girls goodbye. "I must go back to Fairyland, now," she said. "But thank you for saving me and my party bag from the goblin."

"And thank you for all these gorgeous sweets," Rachel replied.

"Goodbye!" called Honey.

And with a final flourish of her wand, and a stream of golden sparkles, she was gone.

"Come on," Rachel turned to Kirsty. "Let's take these to Mrs Twist." The two girls staggered through to the shop with all their Fairyland goodies.

"Goodness, you have done well!" Mrs Twist exclaimed. "Now, let's see…" She peered at one of the jars. "Fizzing Fairies?" she read aloud. "I don't remember buying these." She unscrewed the lid to reveal lots of fairy-shaped sweets, all beautifully wrapped.

Kirsty elbowed Rachel in delight. She was sure she'd just spotted the fairy on the label giving them both a wink.

"Mmmmm," all the boys and girls said, licking their lips as Mrs Twist opened up more of the Fairyland sweets. "These are the best ever!"

Kirsty and Rachel agreed. The marshmallows were soft and fluffy. The liquorice was stretchy and chewy. And the pear drops were scrumptiously tangy.

Kirsty felt something rustle in her pocket. She put her hand in to find a small bag of toffees, carefully tied with a curling gold ribbon. There was a sticker of a honey bee on the front of the bag. And on a label – in gold, shimmering writing – Kirsty read the words "Made with love and honey in Fairyland…"

"Wow," Kirsty breathed. "Look!" Then she smiled. "I think we'd better take these home before I start eating them. Don't they look delicious?"

The two friends said goodbye to Mrs Twist and left the shop.

"Well, that was certainly the tastiest trip to Fairyland yet," Rachel commented.

Kirsty nodded happily. "Just a few days left until the jubilee party," she said. "I can't wait!"

"I hope we get to play Pass the Magic Parcel," Rachel added, laughing as she remembered Polly's game.

Kirsty laughed, too. "One thing's for sure," she said, as she popped a final pear drop into her mouth, "we're definitely going to have sweet dreams tonight!"

Polly
the Party Fun
Fairy

Chapter Five

Polly the Party Fun Fairy

"Goodbye, Mum!" Kirsty Tate called, waving from the mini-bus packed with Brownies as it pulled away from the church hall.

"Goodbye, Mrs Tate!" Rachel shouted, waving too.

As the mini-bus made its way through the village, Rachel turned to Kirsty. "Isn't it great of your Brownie leader to let me come to your mini-jamboree?" she said happily.

"Well, you are a Brownie too," said Kirsty. "Even if you're not in our pack."

Rachel nodded. Both she and Kirsty were wearing their Brownie uniforms. "I'm really looking forward to this," she said eagerly. "What did you do last year?"

"We joined up with another Brownie pack – just like we're doing this time – so there were loads of us," Kirsty explained. "We

played games, ran races, and there were lots of prizes. Then we had a barbecue round the camp fire." She grinned. "It was just a big party in the woods really!"

Rachel's eyes opened wide. "A party?" she gasped. "You know what that means…"

Kirsty clapped a hand to her mouth. "Oh, of course!"

"We'll just have to keep our eyes open," said Rachel, as the mini-bus came to a standstill in a large woodland clearing. There were already lots of Brownies milling around. The other pack had clearly arrived first. "We can't let the goblins get away with any of the Party Fairies' magic party bags."

"And we won't let them spoil our day, either," Kirsty declared, looking determined.

Mrs Talbot, Kirsty's Brownie leader, opened the door of the bus. "Here we are, girls," she said with a smile. "Go and put your bags under that big tree and we'll start with some races."

A cheer went up from the Brownies on the bus as they jumped to their feet. Rachel and Kirsty were the last to clamber out. As they stepped off the bus, they both looked around the clearing.

"There are lots of places for goblins to hide here," Kirsty whispered to Rachel, as they put their bags under the spreading oak tree.

"Gather round, girls," called Mrs Talbot, who had been chatting

with the other Brownie leader, Mrs Carter. "We're going to start with an obstacle race, and we need four volunteers from each pack."

Kirsty nudged Rachel. "That sounds like fun," she said.

Rachel nodded, and they both put their hands up.

"Jenny and Emily," said Mrs Talbot, pointing at two girls. "Oh, and Kirsty and your friend, Rachel – you can be our team!"

Kirsty, Rachel and the other girls watched closely as Mrs Talbot showed them the course of planks, nets and buckets. To finish off, all four members of the team had to jump into a rubber dinghy, and row across the wide stream that flowed along one side of the clearing.

"It looks hard," Kirsty said, nervously.

"Not as hard as trying to outwit goblins!" chuckled Rachel.

As the two teams lined up, the other Brownies began cheering for their teams. Mrs Carter blew her whistle, and they were off!

Jenny ran lightly along a plank first, followed by Rachel and then Kirsty and Emily.

"If anyone falls off, they have to go back to the beginning of the plank and start again!" Mrs Talbot warned. But both teams made it safely across.

Then they began to wriggle under a net. Rachel and Kirsty's team pulled ahead slightly, as one of the Brownies on the other team got her hairclip caught in the mesh.

By the time she was free, Rachel and Kirsty's team had already run along a row of buckets, and was trying to score goals through the netball hoop.

"I'm hopeless at this," Emily said anxiously to Kirsty, as they watched Jenny and then Rachel score with their first shots.

"Don't worry," Kirsty replied. "Just do your best."

But after Kirsty had scored, it took poor Emily six attempts to get her goal. By then, the other team had almost caught up with them.

"Quick, into the dinghy!" Rachel shouted.

They all jumped in and grabbed the paddles. But as they pushed off from the bank, the other team came running over to their boat.

"Paddle harder!" shouted Jenny, as they made their way to the middle of the stream.

Then, suddenly, she felt cold water seeping into her trainers. Surprised, she looked down. Water was pouring into the

boat, and there was the hissing sound of air escaping as the dinghy began to deflate rapidly. It had sprung a leak!

"Girls!" Mrs Talbot was standing on the bank, looking worried. "Are you all right?"

"Our dinghy's leaking!" Kirsty yelled, as they sank even lower in the water.

"So is ours!" shouted the Brownies in the other boat.

"Quickly, girls!" Mrs Carter rolled up her trousers and waded into the stream towards them. "The water's not very deep. Take your shoes and socks off, and climb out."

The eight girls waded to the bank, dragging their now deflated dinghies behind them.

"Do you think this could be goblin mischief?" Kirsty whispered to Rachel.

"It might be," Rachel agreed with a nod.

Mrs Carter was examining one of the dinghies. "Look!" she said, pointing at the rubber. "There are some thorns stuck in there. That's what made the holes. I knew I shouldn't have put the dinghies down next to that gorse bush."

Kirsty and Rachel looked at each other.

"Maybe it was just an accident," Rachel said with a shrug.

"Or maybe a goblin stuck those thorns into the dinghies to make them sink!" Kirsty pointed out.

"Oh, don't worry," Mrs Talbot was saying, patting Mrs Carter comfortingly on the arm. "Let's have the egg and spoon race."

"I'm not very good at this," Kirsty told Rachel as they queued to collect their eggs and spoons. "But it's always good fun."

"It's easier if you don't go too fast," Rachel laughed, "and keep your eye on your egg."

This time all the Brownies took part in the race. Mrs Carter blew the whistle, and they all set off, trying hard not to drop the eggs.

Rachel had a steady hand, so she was soon in the lead, but Kirsty was near the back. Suddenly, Emily rushed past her, trying to catch up with the leaders. Her hand wobbled and her egg fell and smashed on the ground. Immediately, a horrible smell filled the air.

"Ugh!" Emily shrieked, holding her nose. "My egg's rotten!"

"Yuk!" Kirsty exclaimed, covering her nose with her hand. She glanced down at her own egg to check it was steady, but then she noticed something very strange – her egg was beginning to crack!

Kirsty stopped in her tracks and another Brownie almost bumped into her. She stared at the egg as it cracked wide open. The two halves of the shell fell away, leaving a fluffy yellow chick sitting on Kirsty's spoon. It gave a little cheep.

The race was forgotten as the other Brownies crowded round and there was the sound of more eggs cracking. Soon, five other surprised Brownies had chicks sitting on their spoons instead of eggs!

"Well, this is very strange!" said Mrs Carter. "I hard-boiled the eggs for this race. I suppose they must have got mixed up with some uncooked ones."

"Do you think the goblins could have switched the eggs?" Kirsty muttered quietly to Rachel. But before Rachel could reply, Kirsty noticed that her chick had hopped off the spoon and was wandering away. "Hey, come back!" she cried.

Kirsty and Rachel followed Kirsty's chick into the trees.

"There he is," Kirsty said, pointing at the roots of a tree where the chick was pecking around in the soil. Then she looked puzzled. "What's that shimmering light at the bottom of the tree?"

Rachel let out a gasp of delight. "Kirsty, it must be Polly the Party Fun Fairy!" she declared.

Rachel was right. As Kirsty stared at the roots of the tree, Polly the Party Fun Fairy fluttered up into the air, waving her wand happily. She wore a sparkly, blue vest, and matching trousers with

a purple belt and balloon. Long red hair tumbled over her shoulders in untidy, shining waves.

"I'm so glad to see you, girls!" she called in a silvery, bell-like voice, her green eyes gleaming with joy.

"Is everything all right?" asked Kirsty, gently picking up her chick.

Polly looked a bit sad for a moment. "Well, I've lost my party bag," she said, looking round. "I'm sure I put it down here somewhere, but I just can't seem to find it at the moment." She grinned cheekily. "The other Party Fairies say I'm always losing things!"

"Maybe a goblin has stolen it," Rachel suggested. After what had happened so far, she was pretty sure that there was a goblin lurking somewhere. But before she had a chance to convince Polly, they heard Jenny calling from the clearing.

"Kirsty! Rachel! Where are you? We're going to play Frisbee now!"

"You go and play," Polly said with a smile. "I'll carry on looking for my party bag."

"OK, but we'll come and see you again later," Kirsty promised.

Cradling her chick in her hand, she and Rachel hurried back to join the others.

"Pop your chick in here, Kirsty," said Mrs Carter, indicating a large cardboard box. "I'll take all of them to the local farm later. They have a lot of free-range chickens there, so these chicks will have a good home."

Mrs Talbot organised the Brownies into a circle, and they began throwing the Frisbee to each other. It was good fun, and Kirsty and Rachel were enjoying themselves. But at the same time they couldn't help thinking about Polly and her missing party bag.

Suddenly, one of the Brownies tossed the Frisbee very high into the air towards Kirsty. It sailed over Kirsty's head and landed in a bush under the tree where Polly was searching for her party bag.

Kirsty raced off towards the bush. "I'll get that!" she shouted. She couldn't risk Polly being spotted by any of the other Brownies.

"I'll help you look for it," Rachel called, running after her.

Behind them, Mrs Talbot was saying, "Well, that's enough Frisbee for now, girls. Let's have some juice and biscuits."

"Phew, that was close," Kirsty whispered, as she and Rachel stopped underneath the tree. "Where's Polly?"

"Here I am," called a tinkling voice.

The girls looked up, and there was Polly perched on a branch above their heads.

"Did you find your party bag?" asked Rachel.

Polly's shimmering wings drooped a little. "No," she sighed. "But I know where your Frisbee is," she added, pointing down to the middle of a bush.

"Thanks, Polly," said Kirsty. She and Rachel began to push the leaves aside, but as they did so, Polly suddenly cried out in alarm.

"Girls, watch out! There's a goblin!"

There was a loud rustling of leaves as the goblin pushed his way out of the other side of the bush. He had Polly's bright blue party bag in one hand, and the Brownies' Frisbee in the other. Kirsty and Rachel emerged from the bush, just in time to catch a glimpse of him as he raced off.

"Hee-hee," the goblin chuckled gleefully. "A party bag for Jack Frost, and a Frisbee for me. Hurrah!"

"Come back, you horrid goblin!" Polly called crossly. She zoomed after him, her wings fluttering so fast they were a shimmering blur. "Give me back my party bag!"

Polly, Kirsty and Rachel followed the goblin towards the stream.

"We've got him now, girls!" Polly declared triumphantly. "Goblins hate getting their feet wet."

But the goblin wasn't beaten yet.

Panting, he flipped the Frisbee over and launched it onto the water like a little boat. Then he grabbed one of the spoons the Brownies had used in the egg and spoon race and paddled away across the

stream, looking very pleased with himself.

"Thought you'd caught me, didn't you?" he jeered, grinning all over his mean face. "Well, you haven't! Ha, ha, ha!" And he stuck his tongue out at the girls.

"We've got to stop him," Polly said anxiously. "It'll be easier if you two can fly, too." With a wave of her wand and a shower of sparkling fairy dust, Polly turned Kirsty and Rachel into fairies.

"Come on!" yelled Polly, as she skimmed out over the water like a beautiful blue dragonfly.

The goblin looked alarmed and began to row faster.

"How are we going to stop him?"
Kirsty asked Rachel as they flew across
the stream in pursuit.

"I don't know," Rachel replied,
looking round to see if there was
anything to help them.

All of a sudden, Rachel spotted the
row of upturned buckets from the obstacle race.
She turned and flew towards them. Meanwhile, Polly was flying
round the Frisbee-boat, as close to the goblin as she dared, trying
to snatch her party bag back.

"Oh, Polly, be careful!" Kirsty called, wondering where Rachel
had got to.

"Kirsty! Help me!"

Kirsty spun round to see Rachel trying to pick up one of the
buckets. As Rachel was now fairy-sized, she was finding it difficult.
Kirsty fluttered over to help her. "What's this for?" she asked,
helping Rachel lift it up.

"To put over the goblin," Rachel panted.
Carrying the bucket between them,
the two girls flew over the stream.

The goblin had picked up the party
bag now and was holding it tightly,
jabbing at Polly with his spoon to keep
her away.

The two girls hovered above the goblin's
head. "Ready? Now, let go!"

Both girls let go of the bucket at exactly the same moment and it dropped down over the goblin's head, covering him to his knees.

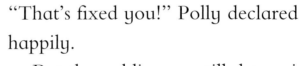

"Help!" the goblin yelled, trying to knock the bucket off. "Everything's gone dark!"

Moaning and groaning to himself, the goblin put the spoon and the party bag down in the bottom of the boat, and began trying to shift the bucket off with both arms. But it was jammed on tight and no matter how much the goblin twisted and turned, he couldn't shake it off.

"That's fixed you!" Polly declared happily.

But the goblin was still determined to get away. He began to paddle again, but because he couldn't see where he was going, he ended up drifting round and round in circles. Polly and the girls laughed.

At the same time, Polly fluttered down and picked up her party bag from the bottom of the boat. "Thank you so much, girls," she beamed, hugging it close.

"No problem," Kirsty said. "But what are we going to do about him?" She pointed at the goblin who was still moaning to himself under the bucket.

"We'd better drag him and the Frisbee to dry land," suggested Rachel.

Polly and the girls took hold of the Frisbee and began towing the goblin towards the bank.

"What are you doing?" the goblin grumbled, "Where are you taking me?"

"You're coming back to Fairyland with me," Polly replied, clutching her party bag tightly.

"Don't want to go to Fairyland," the goblin muttered sulkily.

Rachel and Kirsty couldn't help laughing.

"Well, girls, you've saved the day again," Polly said, flying over to hug them both.

She waved her wand, and a shower of glittering fairy dust swirled through the air and fell over both girls. A few seconds later they were their normal size again.

"Goodbye, Polly," Rachel smiled. "Say hello to the other Party Fairies for us."

But to their surprise, Polly was still hovering in mid-air. "Before I go," she said, "there's just one more thing I need to do…"

She opened her party bag, took out a handful of fairy dust and tossed it into the air. As the sparkling blue dust whirled and tumbled to the ground, Rachel and Kirsty were fascinated to see that it was all in the shape of tiny balloons. Then Polly waved her wand and she and the goblin were gone in a shower of glittering fairy dust.

Kirsty and Rachel looked at each other in wonder, but there wasn't time to think about it now as, at that moment, they heard Mrs Talbot calling. "Kirsty! Rachel! Where are you?"

Kirsty grabbed the Frisbee, and she and Rachel hurried back to join the other Brownies.

"Oh, there you are," said Mrs Talbot. "Here are your juice and biscuits. We're going to play pass the parcel."

"I've got the parcel here," Mrs Carter said, walking towards them with a large parcel wrapped in glittering, multi-coloured paper. "It was on the mini-bus."

Mrs Talbot looked surprised. "That's not the parcel I…" she began doubtfully.

"Well, it must be," said Mrs Carter. "It's the only parcel here."

Rachel and Kirsty glanced at each other and smiled. Now they thought they knew what Polly had been up to when she took the fairy dust out of her party bag and

tossed it in the air – this was a magic parcel from Polly the Party Fun Fairy!

"Come along, girls," called Mrs Carter. "Sit down on the grass in a big circle."

Kirsty and Rachel hurried to join their friends.

Mrs Carter handed the parcel to the nearest Brownie and Mrs Talbot started the music. The Brownies passed the large parcel round the circle. When the music stopped, Jenny was holding the parcel.

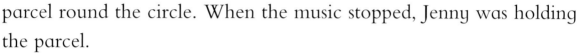

All the Brownies, including Rachel and Kirsty, leaned forward eagerly as she ripped the first layer of paper off.

"Oh!" everyone gasped. Hundreds of clear, shining bubbles were floating up into the air, filling the sky overhead with rainbows. Rachel and Kirsty grinned and nudged one another.

"Look at Mrs Talbot's face," Kirsty whispered, chuckling.

"I'm sure this can't be the parcel I wrapped…" Mrs Talbot was saying, but no one was taking any notice.

Mrs Carter started the music again. This time, when it stopped and a Brownie removed a layer of wrapping, hundreds of pieces of glittering confetti burst out of the paper and floated down onto the grass, disappearing as they landed.

Next, the parcel stopped with a Brownie sitting near Kirsty. She tore a layer of paper off, and everyone gasped as coloured sparkles shot up into the air, then burst overhead like tiny fireworks, filling the sky with dazzling colours.

Just when the girls thought there couldn't be any more surprises, the music stopped again while Rachel was holding the parcel. Taking a deep breath, she pulled the shiny piece of paper apart. It was the last layer. A huge heap of sweets, wrapped in colourful twists of paper, spilled out onto the grass. The Brownies cheered.

"Thank you, Polly," Rachel whispered to herself, as she and Kirsty began to hand the sweets out to the other Brownies.

"We've helped our fairy friends again, and we've had fun, too," Kirsty said, smiling at Rachel. She sighed happily. "Fairy adventures are always the best!"

Phoebe
the Fashion
Fairy

Chapter Six

Phoebe the Fashion Fairy

Kirsty and Rachel were busy wrapping a birthday present for Kirsty's friend, Charlotte.

"There," said Kirsty, tying the ribbon. "She's going to love this silver hairband, it's so pretty."

"Are you nearly ready, girls?" Mrs Tate called up the stairs. "Dad and I have to leave in two minutes!"

"Just coming, Mum," Kirsty replied. Then she turned to Rachel. "I can't believe we're going to another party, can you?" she grinned.

Rachel shook her head. "I wonder what's going to happen this time," she said excitedly.

Kirsty and Rachel put their party dresses into a bag with Charlotte's present, then rushed downstairs.

Kirsty's parents had to go out that afternoon, so Mrs Tate had arranged for the girls to go to Charlotte's house a little early.

As they walked up Charlotte's front path, Rachel couldn't help smiling. "I suspect the goblins won't be able to resist another chance to try and get a magical party bag. One of them is bound to cause trouble."

Kirsty rang the doorbell and a few moments later, Charlotte answered the door.

"Happy birthday!" cried

Kirsty and Rachel together.

But then Kirsty noticed how sad her friend was looking. "Is everything all right?" she asked in concern.

Charlotte didn't seem to be in a birthday mood: she wasn't wearing a party dress and she wasn't even smiling.

"No," she wailed. "Everything is not all right. My best dress has been ruined!"

"Ruined?" Rachel echoed. "How?"

Charlotte held the front door open. "Come upstairs and see," she said miserably.

Kirsty and Rachel gasped when they saw Charlotte's white and gold party dress hanging on her wardrobe door. It had messy splodges of what looked like green paint all over it.

"Oh, no!" Kirsty gasped. "How did that happen?"

Charlotte looked close to tears.

"I don't know," she said. "This morning, it was perfectly clean!"

Charlotte's mum, Mrs Ingle, came in. Her mouth fell open when she saw Charlotte's spoiled dress. "Charlotte!" she exclaimed. "You haven't been painting in your best dress, have you?"

"No," Charlotte cried. "I just came upstairs and found it like this!"

Mrs Ingle frowned. "I hope your brother hasn't had anything to do with it," she said, and marched over to open the window. "Will!" she called down the garden. "Come here at once!"

Charlotte's little brother, Will, scampered into the bedroom a few moments later.

He was covered in mud and looking very pleased with himself. "I found loads of worms," he told the girls happily, brandishing a small muddy spade.

"Will, your sister's party is starting soon," Mrs Ingle groaned. "You were supposed to be getting ready."

Will glanced over at Charlotte. "Well, Charlotte isn't ready yet – and it's her party!" he protested.

"Speaking of which," Mrs Ingle went on, "do you know anything about this?"

She showed Will Charlotte's party dress and he shook his head vigorously.

"I've been in the garden all morning!" he insisted. Charlotte nodded. "It's true, Mum," she said. "I saw him."

Mrs Ingle sighed. "Well, I suppose the dress must have brushed against something," she said, looking baffled.

Rachel and Kirsty glanced around the room uneasily. Both girls knew it was just the sort of thing a goblin would do. And the green paint on the dress was an unmistakeable goblin green.

Mrs Ingle looked at her watch. "We've got one hour before the party starts," she said "We could pop round to the dry-cleaner's and see if they can help, but I've still got the fairy cakes to ice."

"We'll ice the cakes for you while you're out," Kirsty suggested.

Mrs Ingle smiled. "That's very kind of you, girls," she said. "Are you sure you wouldn't mind?"

"Of course not. It will be fun," Kirsty replied at once.

Mrs Ingle led the girls downstairs. Then, while Mr Ingle whisked Will away to get him cleaned up, Mrs Ingle took Rachel and Kirsty into the dining room, where the party food had all been laid out on the table.

"One tray of fairy cakes, one bowl of icing, a piping bag and some cake decorations," she said, setting them out. "This is really helpful, girls. Thank you!"

Then Charlotte and her mum hurried off to the dry-cleaner's with Charlotte's ruined dress.

As soon as Kirsty and Rachel heard Mrs Ingle's car leave the driveway, they looked at each other meaningfully.

"We've got to find that goblin," Kirsty said in a low voice, "before he does anything else to spoil the party."

"Well, he must have been in Charlotte's bedroom not so long ago. Let's go back up and see if he's still there," Rachel suggested.

The girls made their way upstairs to Charlotte's room. Kirsty put her finger to her lips, then crept up to the wardrobe and flung the doors wide open.

But there was no sign of the goblin in Charlotte's wardrobe, so Kirsty peered under the bed while Rachel checked behind the curtains.

Then Rachel looked beneath Charlotte's duvet and Kirsty checked on top of all the cupboards.

Rachel sighed. "He could be anywhere in the house by now," she said.

Kirsty glanced at her watch. "Come on, we'd better get on with those cakes," she said.

"Otherwise we'll be the ones spoiling Charlotte's party."

Downstairs, Kirsty and Rachel began icing the cakes, trying to think where the goblin might be hiding. Kirsty piped heart shapes onto each cake, while Rachel decorated them with hundreds and thousands.

Rachel was just finishing the last cake when Kirsty nudged her. "Look!" she urged.

Rachel looked up to see a stream of tiny, sparkly, red hearts floating past the window.

Both girls ran over to take a closer look. There, waving at them through the glass, was a beautiful, smiling fairy!

"It's Phoebe the Fashion Fairy!" Rachel cried, opening the window for her.

Phoebe had long, wavy hair, held back by a crimson Alice band. She wore a little white dress with a row of red hearts around the hem and matching shoes. Her scarlet wand had a ruby heart at one end that glittered in the sunlight.

She fluttered inside and perched on the windowsill. "Hello!" she said in a bright, silvery voice. "Kirsty and Rachel, isn't it? I remember seeing you when Honey the Sweet Fairy showed you around the Party Fairy workshop."

"That's right," Kirsty said. "And I remember your gorgeous fashion department, with all those wonderful, sparkly fairy dresses."

Phoebe nodded and then looked serious. "Now, I heard that there was a party dress disaster here, so I've come to work a little bit of fairy magic and sort everything out."

"Well, we're very glad to see you," Kirsty said, and quickly filled Phoebe in on what had happened to Charlotte's dress.

Phoebe's delicate features creased into a frown. "That does sound like goblin mischief," she agreed. "We'll have to be careful."

"We'll just clear these icing things away," Rachel said, "and then we'll show you where Charlotte's bedroom is."

Kirsty arranged the fairy cakes on a plate while Rachel started gathering up the icing equipment. Phoebe fluttered over for a closer look at the cakes.

Rachel was frowning. "Where's the icing bag?" she asked Kirsty. "I can't see it anywhere."

Kirsty looked round. "It was there a moment ago," she said, pointing to one end of the table.

"I know," Rachel agreed, sounding puzzled. "But it's vanished."

No sooner had she said these words, than the lid of Will's toybox flew back with a loud crash. The girls and Phoebe spun around to see a goblin bursting out of the toy chest like a grinning, green jack-in-the-box.

"It's the goblin!" Kirsty cried.

"With the piping bag!" Rachel added.

The goblin held up the piping bag and squeezed it hard. A jet of icing shot out and hit Phoebe right in the tummy!

"Help!" she cried in surprise, tumbling backwards.

Kirsty and Rachel watched in horror as Phoebe fell. Luckily, she landed in the big, soft jelly in the middle of the table and then bounced up into the air again, arms flailing as she tried to recover her balance.

SQUELCH! Back into the jelly, Phoebe plunged. She was

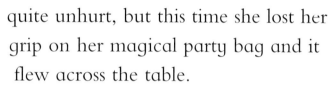

quite unhurt, but this time she lost her grip on her magical party bag and it flew across the table.

"Just what I was after," the goblin chortled, leaping out of the toybox.

Rachel gasped. "Oh, no, you don't!" she cried, dashing round the table to try and reach the party bag before the goblin could take it.

But she was too late. And the goblin's gnarly, green hand closed

around Phoebe's shimmering party bag, seconds before Rachel could get to it.

The goblin grinned nastily, snatched up a fairy cake in his other hand, and leapt out of the window into the garden.

"Oh, no!" Phoebe gasped, struggling out of the sticky jelly. "I need my party bag or I won't be able to fix Charlotte's dress!" Phoebe waved her wand. Sparkling red hearts streamed from the tip and spilled all over Kirsty and Rachel. "I'll make you fairy-sized," she said. "Then we can all fly after that goblin thief."

Kirsty and Rachel shut their eyes in delight as Phoebe's magic got to work and they felt themselves shrinking. Beautiful, shimmering fairy wings appeared on their backs, and Rachel couldn't resist flying a little loop-the-loop.

Phoebe fluttered out of the window and the girls followed. They could see the goblin running down the garden, greedily stuffing the fairy cake into his mouth as he went.

He glanced over his shoulder and spotted the three fairies zooming after him. A look of panic crossed his face and he glanced around wildly, searching for somewhere to hide. The next moment he spotted the Wendy House and dived inside, slamming the door.

Phoebe was first to reach him. She knocked loudly. "Let me in!" she ordered crossly.

"There's nobody home!" called the goblin from inside.

Phoebe sighed and tried to pull the door open, but the goblin must have been holding tight to the handle on the other side, for it didn't move.

"It's no good, I'm not strong enough," Phoebe wailed.

"If you turn us back into girls, we might be able to do it," Kirsty suggested.

"Good idea," Phoebe said, waving her wand again to release another stream of red hearts.

Kirsty and Rachel felt their arms and legs tingling with fairy magic as they grew back to their normal size.

"Right!" Rachel said, grabbing hold of the door handle. "Let's get this door open."

There was a scraping sound from inside the Wendy House and then, to Rachel's dismay, she found that she couldn't even turn the handle.

"The goblin must have wedged something under the door handle," she cried in frustration. "A chair or something – it won't budge at all now!"

Phoebe groaned. "What are we going to do?" she asked anxiously.

Kirsty, Rachel and Phoebe stared around the garden, wondering what to try next. Rachel spotted the garden hose and her eyes lit up as a thought popped into her head. "How about this?" she asked the other two. "We put the end of the hose down the chimney, turn the tap on, and flood that nasty goblin out of the Wendy House!"

Kirsty chuckled. "I love it!" she said.

Phoebe was smiling too as Kirsty quickly dangled the end of the hosepipe down the Wendy House chimney, while Rachel ran to turn on the outside tap. A few moments later, there came a great SPLASH! – quickly followed by a surprised yelp from the goblin.

"Where's that rain coming from?" he grumbled. "I'm getting wet."

More water splashed into the Wendy House and the goblin's moans got louder. "Make it stop!" he groaned.

"We'll make it stop if you come out and give Phoebe her party bag," Kirsty offered.

"Shan't!" the goblin retorted rudely. "This party bag is mine now, and I'm going to give it to Jack Frost!"

"Well, you can't say we didn't warn you, goblin," Rachel shouted, racing over to turn the tap on fully. "Here comes the flood!"

Water poured into the Wendy House in torrents. Through the window, the girls and Phoebe could see the goblin bobbing helplessly around as the water level rose.

Then he floated against the small chair he'd used to wedge the door shut. The chair was knocked aside and the Wendy House door flew open.

"Help!" cried the goblin, as a huge wave of water gushed out of the Wendy House door, carrying him along on top of it.

"I didn't know goblins could surf!" Kirsty laughed as he sailed past her. She stretched out an arm and snatched Phoebe's party bag from his hands. "Got it!" she declared happily, passing the bag to Phoebe.

The goblin shrieked and flapped about in the river of water, trying to get to his feet. But it was impossible, the rushing stream carried him all the way down the garden and straight into the pond.

Kirsty, Rachel and Phoebe couldn't help laughing as they watched the goblin clamber out, dripping wet and with a huge clump of duckweed plastered to his head.

"I'm almost tempted to magic him a special outfit," Phoebe chuckled. "Some swimming trunks, goggles and a nice, flowery swimming hat!"

The goblin stomped away, defeated.

"I think that's the last we'll see of our soggy friend today," Kirsty said with a grin.

Rachel ran to turn the tap off, and then waved frantically at Phoebe and Kirsty. "Mrs Ingle's back with Charlotte!" she hissed. "I just heard the car!"

Kirsty's face fell. Not only was the garden a mud-bath now, but the Wendy House was a mess, the jelly was ruined, and she and Rachel were all wet, too! How on earth were they going to explain everything to Mrs Ingle?

"Leave it to me," Phoebe said quickly. "You keep Charlotte's mum talking. I'll fix the Wendy House and then the dining room. Now, hurry!"

Kirsty and Rachel ran into the house to find poor Charlotte looking more upset than ever. "The cleaners said they'd never seen anything like this paint," she explained sadly. "They tried all sorts of things to get it off my dress but nothing would shift it."

Mrs Ingle put a comforting arm around her daughter. "Never mind," she said. "You've got lots of other nice things to wear. You'll just have to choose something else."

She glanced over at Kirsty and Rachel, as Charlotte began to trudge upstairs. "And you two should change, too," Mrs Ingle went on. "The party's going to start any minute."

A puzzled frown appeared between her eyebrows as she took in Rachel and Kirsty's damp clothes. "You look rather wet. Are you all right?" she asked.

"Um…" Kirsty began, not sure how to explain her bedraggled appearance.

"We're fine," Rachel put in hastily.

"We just got a bit splashed when we were washing up the icing things, that's all."

Mrs Ingle's frown cleared. "I'd completely forgotten about the fairy cakes," she said. "Did you get them all finished?" She walked 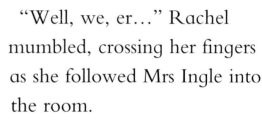 towards the dining room door.

"Well, we, er…" Rachel mumbled, crossing her fingers as she followed Mrs Ingle into the room.

Could Phoebe possibly have had time to magic the Wendy House back to normal and sort out the dining room?

Kirsty and Rachel shouldn't have worried; clever Phoebe had worked wonders! The fairy cakes were neatly arranged on their plate once more, and the jelly was its perfect wobbly self again.

Kirsty blinked as she noticed a tiny glimmer of sparkly red light

 The Party Fairies Treasury

flicker around the table, then vanish quickly. She turned to Rachel questioningly, and Rachel nodded. She had seen it, too.

A last sparkle of fairy magic!

Luckily, Mrs Ingle had noticed no such thing: she was too busy admiring the fairy cakes.

"You are clever, girls," she said. "I couldn't have decorated them more beautifully myself – thank you so much."

"You're welcome," Kirsty said, smiling with relief. "Now, we'd better go and get changed."

Just then, there was an excited cry from upstairs. "Kirsty, Rachel! Come quickly!"

Kirsty and Rachel rushed up to Charlotte's room. To their amazement, hanging on the wardrobe door were three gorgeous party dresses. One was a beautiful deep red, all covered in golden hearts, with a matching hairband. A tag hanging from the sleeve said 'Charlotte' in pretty, sparkly writing.

The other two dresses had tags that read 'Kirsty' and 'Rachel'.

Kirsty's dress was pink with a lilac dragonfly embroidered near the hem, and Rachel's dress was lilac with pink butterflies around the neckline.

"This is the most

beautiful dress ever," Charlotte breathed, stroking the shimmering red material. "But where did it come from?"

Rachel opened her mouth but couldn't think of a single thing to say.

"Happy birthday, Charlotte!" Kirsty cried, thinking quickly. "It's our present to you. We, er, went and got it while you were out – just in case the cleaners couldn't fix your dress."

"And here's a little something else, as well," Rachel added, pulling the present they'd wrapped up earlier out of the bag. "Happy birthday!"

"Oh, thank you!" Charlotte cried happily, hugging both girls.

As Charlotte started opening the present, Kirsty suddenly nudged Rachel.

Rachel turned to see what her friend had spotted. To her delight, the dragonfly and butterflies on their party dresses were fluttering their delicate embroidered wings and twinkling with golden lights. She grinned at Kirsty.

Charlotte was pulling off the last bit of wrapping paper. "What a gorgeous necklace!" she exclaimed, holding it up. "I love it."

Kirsty and Rachel stared. The silver hairband they'd wrapped up for Charlotte back at Kirsty's house had been turned into a gleaming golden necklace with three, heart-shaped beads strung in the middle.

Phoebe's work again, Kirsty thought, smiling.

Charlotte pulled on her dress and Rachel fastened the necklace around her neck.

"I must go and show Mum," Charlotte said, twirling around happily. "Thank you so much. This is turning out to be the best birthday I've ever had!"

As soon as Charlotte had left the room, Phoebe peeped out from behind a curtain. With a smile, she waved her wand, and Kirsty and Rachel suddenly found themselves wearing their new party dresses, while their old clothes were neatly folded in piles on the bed.

"Oh, Phoebe, these dresses are just gorgeous," Kirsty declared, standing in front of the mirror. "Thank you!"

Phoebe's cheeks blushed pink. "Oh, it's nothing," she said, looking terribly pleased. "I'm just doing my job. Happy to help!" Then she smiled. "Anyway, I should be thanking you for saving my party bag from the goblin."

"Oh, it's nothing," Kirsty grinned.

"Happy to help," Rachel laughed.

"Just doing our job!" they chorused.

Phoebe came over and hugged them.

"Have a lovely party," she said. "I must fly back to Fairyland now."

Kirsty and Rachel waved goodbye as Phoebe disappeared in a swirl of glittering fairy dust.

Then the doorbell rang downstairs. "Charlotte's friends are here," Kirsty said happily. "Let's go and have some fun. I think we've earned it today."

"We certainly have," Rachel agreed. "And I can't wait for our next adventure!"

Jasmine
the Present Fairy

Chapter Seven

Jasmine the Present Fairy

"Look at all these stalls, Rachel," Kirsty Tate said, pointing down the street where she lived. "This is going to be a great party!"

All of Kirsty's neighbours were bustling around setting up stalls outside their houses. There were all sorts of things going on, from games and raffles to stalls selling bric-a-brac and cakes. Delicious smells wafted towards the girls from the barbecue at the other end of the street. The road was closed to traffic, and people were already milling around in the sunshine, enjoying the fête.

"I think having a street party is a great idea," Rachel said with a grin. "I wish we had one in our street back home. Shall we explore?"

"Good idea!" Kirsty answered, as they set off to wander through the crowds. "It'll give us a chance to look for goblins!"

"We could have a go on the tombola." Kirsty pointed to where the tombola was manned by one of Kirsty's neighbours, Mr Cooper. There was already a queue. Kirsty and Rachel stood behind a little girl holding her mum's hand.

The girl was staring up at the prizes on the shelves behind the tombola machine. "I hope I win a cuddly toy, Mummy," she said excitedly.

"Any ticket ending in four wins a prize!" called Mr Cooper, spinning the tombola round.

Rachel and Kirsty watched as the little girl pulled out a purple ticket. She unfolded it carefully.

"Mummy, I won!" she gasped. "It's number 214."

"Well done!" her mum laughed.

"Let's hope it's a soft toy," Rachel whispered to Kirsty, as the little girl handed Mr Cooper the ticket.

But sharp-eyed Kirsty had already spotted the prize with purple ticket 214 pinned to it. "It's not," she said, pointing. "Look."

The prize was a blue plastic apron with a picture of a fluffy, white kitten on the front. Kirsty hoped the little girl wouldn't be too disappointed.

"Right, let me find your prize," said Mr Cooper, scanning the shelves. "It's here somewhere…"

But just before he spotted the apron, something magical happened. Rachel and Kirsty saw a shower of blue sparkles appear from thin air and whirl around the apron. The next moment, the apron had vanished and in its place sat a fluffy, white toy kitten, with a blue satin bow around its neck. Pinned to the bow was purple ticket 214.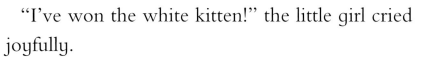

"I've won the white kitten!" the little girl cried joyfully.

Looking puzzled, Mr Cooper lifted the toy down. "I don't remember seeing that prize before," he murmured.

Kirsty and Rachel grinned at each other as Mr Cooper handed the kitten to the delighted little girl.

"There must be a Party Fairy very nearby!" said Rachel.

The little girl skipped off happily, clutching her prize, while Kirsty and Rachel slipped behind the tombola stall to look for the fairy. They couldn't see any sign of her.

"Rachel! Kirsty!" The girls suddenly heard a silvery voice calling from above their heads. "I'm up here!"

The girls looked up at a string of coloured flags tied to the top of the stall, and there was Jasmine the Present Fairy, balancing on the string like an acrobat on a tightrope!

"Hello," Kirsty and Rachel called, smiling up at her.

Jasmine fluttered down to join them, her straight brown hair flying out behind her. She wore a long, blue skirt with a fluted hemline that swirled around her ankles, and a cropped top in the same shade of blue. On her feet were dark blue ballet shoes with satin ribbons, and in her hand she carried a glittering blue wand.

"I'm here to make sure that your street party goes well," she explained, "and that all the prizes are as perfect as possible." She smiled at Rachel and Kirsty.

"Have you seen any goblins?" Rachel asked anxiously.

"No—" Jasmine began, but she was interrupted by the sound of someone crying loudly. It came from the lucky dip, next to the tombola.

"Someone sounds upset," Kirsty whispered. "Maybe we'd better take a look."

Jasmine flew down and hid on Rachel's shoulder behind her hair.

Then they hurried over to join the queue at the lucky dip. A little

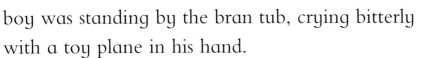

boy was standing by the bran tub, crying bitterly with a toy plane in his hand.

"I loved the plane when I unwrapped it," the boy wailed. "But look, Dad, the wings are broken!"

"This could be goblin trouble," Jasmine whispered in Rachel's ear.

"I'm very sorry," said the man at the lucky dip stall. "I tell you what, why don't you pull out another parcel for free?"

The boy stopped crying immediately. "Thank you," he beamed. Rachel, Kirsty and Jasmine watched as the little boy put his hand into the bran tub and pulled out a small parcel. He unwrapped it eagerly, but they all stared in horror when a mouldy, old apple fell out!

"Oh, no!" Jasmine gasped.

The little boy began to cry again.

Meanwhile, the stallholder was looking very flustered. "I think somebody's playing a silly joke on me!" he said crossly. "Don't cry." He patted the little boy on the shoulder.

"All the presents in the lucky dip are spoiled," Kirsty whispered to Rachel and Jasmine. "What are we going to do?"

The little boy was about to burst into tears again, but the kind stallholder saved the day.

"Look," he said, leaning across to the hook-a-duck stall next door, which he was also running. "I'll give you one of these prizes instead." And he handed the boy a shiny bat and ball set.

"Great!" the boy said happily, showing it to his dad as they walked away.

"I'll soon set things right with my party magic," said Jasmine.

While the man was talking to Rachel, Jasmine slid quietly off her shoulder and flew down to the edge of the bran tub. Meanwhile, Kirsty stood right in front of the tub so that nobody in the queue could see what was happening.

Quickly, Jasmine opened her party bag and took out a handful of sparkling blue fairy dust, shaped like tiny bows. She sprinkled it over the bran tub and gave a sigh of relief. "All done!" she whispered to Kirsty.

But just then there was a scrabbling noise from the bran tub. Suddenly, a big green goblin popped up and snatched at Jasmine's party bag.

"Oh!" Jasmine and Kirsty gasped together as the goblin lunged towards them.

Luckily, Jasmine was too quick for him and she whisked the party bag out of his reach.

Muttering crossly, the goblin leapt out of the bran tub and darted out of sight behind the stall.

Still shaking with fright, Jasmine fluttered up to sit on Kirsty's shoulder but as she landed, her party bag slipped from her trembling fingers. It fell straight into the lucky dip and disappeared amidst the sawdust.

"Oh, no!" Kirsty groaned.

Over the shoulder of the stallholder, Rachel had seen what was happening. Somehow they had to get Jasmine's party bag back – and fast. "Er, can I have a go on the lucky dip?" she asked.

The man looked amazed. "Are you sure?" he asked. "It doesn't seem very lucky at the moment."

"Quite sure," Rachel said firmly.

"Me too," Kirsty added, guessing what Rachel was up to.

The two girls handed over their money. Kirsty went first and Rachel, Jasmine and the stallholder watched as she felt around inside the tub. Her fingers closed over something and she pulled it out. But it was one of the wrapped presents, not Jasmine's party bag. Inside the parcel was a beautiful blue mini-kite.

"At least the presents are OK now," Jasmine whispered in Kirsty's ear.

"Your turn," said the stallholder, looking at Rachel. But just then one of the children at the hook-a-duck stall gave a cry of alarm. He had accidentally got his fishing-rod caught in a string of flags! The stallholder went to help, and Rachel leaned over the bran tub.

But just as Rachel was making her lucky dip, Kirsty gave a gasp of horror.

"Watch out!" she whispered. "The goblin is climbing up the table leg!"

Sure enough, the goblin was clambering up the leg of the table back towards the bran tub, with a very determined look on his face.

"There's only your dip left, Rachel," Kirsty whispered anxiously. "You must get Jasmine's party bag before the goblin does!"

Quickly, Rachel plunged her hand into the sawdust and began to feel around. She wondered how she would know when she'd found the party bag, but then she felt something tingle under her fingers. "Fairy magic!" Rachel said to herself, as she drew Jasmine's party bag out.

"Hurrah!" Jasmine cried happily. "Thanks, Rachel."

"Let's get out of here," Kirsty suggested. "Quick, back to my house!"

The girls and Jasmine darted behind the stall and ran away from the fête towards the Tates' house but the goblin started chasing them.

Rachel glanced over her shoulder. "He's not far behind!" she panted.

They reached the house and Kirsty let them in through the front door. But the goblin was charging towards them and the girls only

just managed to slam the door shut in time.

"I've got an idea," Kirsty declared suddenly. "Rachel, you guard the door. Jasmine, follow me."

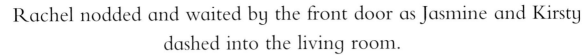

Rachel nodded and waited by the front door as Jasmine and Kirsty dashed into the living room.

Then a tiny sound made Rachel jump. Her heart thumping, Rachel looked round. She smiled to see Pearl, Kirsty's black and white kitten, sitting at the top of the stairs, watching her.

But then Rachel heard something else. It was the noise of the catflap in the kitchen door creaking open. Rachel frowned. Who was coming in?

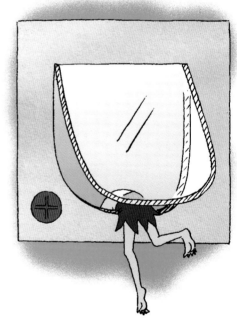

She crept along the hall towards the kitchen and spotted…the goblin, climbing in through the catflap.

"Kirsty! Jasmine!" she shouted. "Look out, the goblin's coming!"

In the living-room, Jasmine looked at Kirsty in alarm. "What shall we do?" she cried.

But Kirsty was picking up an empty cardboard box which had been full of books for the stall. "If we can make the goblin believe

your party bag is in this box, we might be able to trap him inside!" she said. "Can you lay a trail of magic sparkles leading into the box?"

"I can do better than that!" Jasmine replied eagerly.

She opened her party bag and sprinkled some glittering fairy dust onto the cardboard. Immediately, it changed into a beautiful blue gift box, with a lovely red ribbon lying beside it. Then Jasmine laid the trail of fairy dust into the box and she and Kirsty dived out of sight behind the sofa.

No sooner were Kirsty and Jasmine in hiding than the goblin dashed into the living-room and skidded to a halt, closely followed by Rachel.

"Oh, no!" she gasped. "If the party bag is in the box, the goblin can take it!"

The goblin had also spotted the fairy dust trail and he was beaming all over his face.

"Ha!" he chuckled gleefully, sticking his tongue out at Rachel. "Jack Frost is going to be very pleased with me when I take him a magic party bag!"

And, still chuckling, he crawled into the box.

Immediately, Jasmine and Kirsty rushed out from behind the sofa. Rachel, who wasn't expecting it, almost jumped out of her skin.

"Quick, Rachel!" cried Kirsty, "Help me close the box!"

Rachel sprang forward, and she and Kirsty shut the lid.

Then Jasmine waved her wand, and the gold ribbon floated up into the air and tied itself firmly around the box.

There was a cry of rage from inside as the goblin realised he'd been tricked.

"So that's what you were up to!" Rachel laughed.

"Let me out!" the goblin roared.

"I don't think so," Kirsty replied.

"Shall we send the goblin back to Jack Frost by fairy magic mail?" Jasmine suggested.

The girls nodded and Jasmine waved her wand again. There was a shower of fairy dust and a label appeared on the box. It said "Jack Frost, Ice Castle" in big letters. Then, in another swirl of glittering magic, the parcel vanished completely.

Kirsty turned to Rachel. "We did it!" she beamed. "We've saved all the Party Fairies' magic party bags!"

"That means the jubilee party for our king and queen can go ahead without any more trouble from Jack Frost," Jasmine declared happily. "And it's all thanks to you two."

Kirsty and Rachel grinned proudly at each other.

Then Kirsty stared. "Look!" she cried, pointing at the window.

A rainbow of shimmering colours was streaming through the glass. The girls blinked in wonder as one end of the beautiful rainbow came to rest on the floor beside them.

"It's the magic rainbow to take us to Fairyland!" Rachel breathed.

"Oh!" Kirsty gasped. "But we're not ready! We haven't got our party clothes on."

Jasmine laughed. "Just step onto the end of the rainbow, girls," she told them. "We Party Fairies will soon sort you out when you get to Fairyland." She waved her wand. "See you very soon!" she called, as she vanished in a swirl of glitter.

"Come on, Kirsty," Rachel said, taking her friend's hand.

Together, the girls stepped carefully onto the rainbow. Immediately, there was a whooshing sound, and they were surrounded by glittering golden fairy dust as the rainbow whisked them away.

"Here they are!" called a joyful voice.

As the golden sparkles cleared, the girls found themselves in the Great Hall of the Party Workshop in Fairyland. They were already fairy-sized themselves, with glittering wings on their backs. And there was Jasmine and the other six Party Fairies smiling at them.

"Welcome to the party!" they cried.

"Wow!" Rachel exclaimed, looking round.

Last time the girls had been there, the Party Fairies had been busy with preparations, but now everything was ready.

"I'm so happy to see you, girls," the Fairy Godmother declared as she hurried towards them. She turned to Phoebe the Fashion Fairy. "I think Phoebe has something for you."

"I do!" Phoebe laughed. "How about some beautiful new dresses for the party, girls?"

"Oh, yes please!" Kirsty and Rachel cried together.

Phoebe smiled and threw a handful of sparkling fairy dust over them. Both girls closed their eyes.

Kirsty was the first to open them again. "Oh, Rachel!" she gasped. "These are the most beautiful dresses I've ever seen!"

Rachel opened her eyes to see Kirsty wearing a long, sparkling rose-pink and gold dress, with pink ballet shoes and a glittering pink tiara. Rachel wore the same, but her outfit was in shimmering lilac and silver.

"Thank you, Phoebe—" the girls began.

But before they could say any more, a little fairy zoomed into the Great Hall, panting with excitement. "The king and queen are here!" she cried.

Rachel, Kirsty and all the fairies crowded around the door.

A shining crystal carriage, pulled by six white unicorns and driven by Bertram, the frog footman, was making its way towards them. The carriage stopped and out stepped the Fairy king and queen.

"SURPRISE!" shouted everybody.

The king and queen looked puzzled for a moment, but then they saw the golden banner which hung over the castle door: Congratulations to our beloved King Oberon and Queen Titania on their 1000th jubilee!

"Oh!" the queen gasped, looking delighted. "How wonderful!"

"I think our Party Fairies have had a hand in this," the king beamed joyfully.

The Fairy Godmother stepped forward. "Welcome, King Oberon and Queen Titania!" she announced. "The Party Fairies aren't the only ones who have helped to make this party special. We must also thank our friends, Rachel and Kirsty." And she turned to smile at the girls. "Once again they have saved us from Jack Frost's mischief."

"Thank you, girls," said the king warmly. "You must tell us the whole story later."

"You both look beautiful," the queen added with a smile.

"Now, let's forget all about Jack Frost, and enjoy the party!"

Rachel and Kirsty had never been to such a party in their lives. The frog orchestra played catchy tunes, specially created by Melodie the Music Fairy, and all the fairies danced and fluttered around like colourful butterflies.

Then there were party games, organised by Polly the Party Fun Fairy: Pass the Magic Parcel, Musical Magical Chairs and many more.

The sweets made by Honey the Sweet Fairy were so delicious that Rachel and Kirsty just couldn't stop eating the Strawberry Sparkles.

After the games, everyone gathered round to watch the king and queen open their presents and then cut the wonderful cake, made by Cherry and iced by the goblin. All too soon, the party was over.

"I hope you've had a good time, girls," Queen Titania said, smiling at Rachel and Kirsty.

"It was great!" Rachel declared.

"The best party ever!" Kirsty added.

"It's time for you to go home now," the queen went on. She waved her wand and a shimmering rainbow appeared beside them.

"But before you go, I think the Party Fairies have something for you."

Jasmine and Cherry flew forward.

"These are from all of us!" Jasmine said, handing Kirsty a pink, sparkly party bag, while Cherry gave Rachel a lilac one. "Don't look in them till you get home."

"Thank you," Kirsty and Rachel replied, waving at their friends. "See you again soon, we hope."

"Goodbye!" answered all the fairies.

And with the voices of their fairy friends ringing in their ears, the girls stepped into the rainbow. Moments later, they found themselves in the Tates' kitchen, restored to their usual size and wearing their normal clothes once more.

"Oh, that was magical!" Kirsty sighed happily.

Rachel was already opening her party bag. "Look, Kirsty!" she exclaimed in delight.

The bags were full of presents from their Party Fairy friends. There was a piece of jubilee cake from Cherry, a fairy music CD from Melodie, a tub of glittery lip gloss from Grace, a silk bag of sweets from Honey, a pack of magic playing cards from Polly and a sparkly bracelet from Phoebe.

And Jasmine had given them each a golden jewellery box with a revolving fairy on top to put all their presents in.

"We must be the luckiest girls in the world," Rachel sighed.

"And we can still enjoy the rest of the street party, too," Kirsty added.

Later that night, the girls lay in their beds in Kirsty's room, still too excited to sleep.

"It's sad that I have to go home tomorrow," Rachel said with a yawn. "But I've really enjoyed our latest fairy adventure."

"Me too," Kirsty agreed, starting to feel sleepy at last. She closed her eyes.

There was silence for a few moments. Then, "I can hear something,"

Rachel said. "It's coming from our jewellery boxes!"

The soft, tinkling sound of party music filled the room.

"Fairy magic!" Kirsty said happily, snuggling down under her duvet. "Goodnight, Rachel."

Meet all the Rainbow Magic fairies in these exciting storybooks!

The Rainbow Fairies

Ruby the Red Fairy – 978-1-84362-0167
Amber the Orange Fairy – 978-1-84362-0174
Saffron the Yellow Fairy – 978-1-84362-0181
Fern the Green Fairy – 978-1-84362-0198
Sky the Blue Fairy – 978-1-84362-0204
Izzy the Indigo Fairy – 978-1-84362-0211
Heather the Violet Fairy – 978-1-84362-0228

The Weather Fairies

Crystal the Snow Fairy – 978-1-84362-633-6
Abigail the Breeze Fairy – 978-1-84362-634-3
Pearl the Cloud Fairy – 978-1-84362-635-0
Goldie the Sunshine Fairy – 978-1-84362-641-1
Evie the Mist Fairy – 978-1-84362-636-7
Storm the Lightning Fairy – 978-1-84362-637-4
Hayley the Rain Fairy – 978-1-84362-638-1

The Party Fairies

Cherry the Cake Fairy – 978-1-84362-818-7
Melodie the Music Fairy – 978-1-84362-819-4
Grace the Glitter Fairy – 978-1-84362-820-0
Honey the Sweet Fairy – 978-1-84362-821-7
Polly the Party Fun Fairy – 978-184362-822-4
Phoebe the Fashion Fairy – 978-184362-823-1
Jasmine the Present Fairy – 978-1-84362-824-8

The Jewel Fairies

India the Moonstone Fairy – 978-1-84362-958-0
Scarlett the Garnet Fairy – 978-1-84362-954-2
Emily the Emerald Fairy – 978-1-84362-955-9
Chloe the Topaz Fairy – 978-1-84362-956-6
Amy the Amethyst Fairy – 978-1-84362-957-3
Sophie the Sapphire Fairy – 978-184362-953-5
Lucy the Diamond Fairy – 978-1-84362-959-7

The Pet Keeper Fairies

Katie the Kitten Fairy – 978-1-84616-166-7
Bella the Bunny Fairy – 978-1-84616-170-4
Georgia the Guinea Pig Fairy – 978-1-84616-168-1
Lauren the Puppy Fairy – 978-1-84616-169-8
Harriet the Hamster Fairy – 978-1-84616-167-4
Molly the Goldfish Fairy – 978-1-84616-172-8
Penny the Pony Fairy – 978-1-84616-171-1

The Fun Day Fairies

Megan the Monday Fairy – 978-1-84616-188-9
Tallulah the Tuesday Fairy – 978-1-84616-189-6
Willow the Wednesday Fairy – 978-1-84616-190-2
Thea the Thursday Fairy – 978-1-84616-191-9
Freya the Friday Fairy – 978-1-84616-192-6
Sienna the Saturday Fairy – 978-1-84616-193-3
Sarah the Sunday Fairy – 978-1-84616-194-0

The Petal Fairies

Tia the Tulip Fairy – 978-1-84616-457-6
Pippa the Poppy Fairy – 978-1-84616-458-3
Louise the Lily Fairy – 978-1-84616-459-0
Charlotte the Sunflower Fairy – 978-184616-460-6
Danielle the Daisy Fairy – 978-1-84616-462-0
Olivia the Orchid Fairy – 978-1-84616-461-3
Ella the Rose Fairy – 978-1-84616-464-4

The Dance Fairies

Bethany the Ballet Fairy- 978-1-84616-490-3
Jade the Disco Fairy – 978-1-84616-491-0
Rebecca the Rock 'N 'Roll Fairy -978-1-84616-492-7
Tasha the Tap Dance Fairy – 978-1-84616-493-4
Jessica the Jazz Fairy – 978-1-84616-495-8
Saskia the Salsa Fairy – 978-1-84616-496-5
Imogen the Ice Dance Fairy – 978-1-84616-497-2

The Sporty Fairies

Helena the Horseriding Fairy – 978-1-84616-888-8
Francesca the Football Fairy – 978-1-84616-889-5
Zoe the Skating Fairy – 978-1-84616-890-1
Naomi the Netball Fairy – 978-1-84616-891-8
Samantha the Swimming Fairy – 978-184616-892-5
Alice the Tennis Fairy – 978-184616-893-2
Gemma the Gymnastics Fairy – 978-184616-894-9

The Music Fairies

Poppy the Piano Fairy – 978-140830-033-6
Ellie the Guitar Fairy – 978-140830-030-5
Fiona the Flute Fairy – 978-140830-029-9
Danni the Drum Fairy – 978-140830-028-2
Maya the Harp Fairy – 978-1-40830-031-2
Victoria the Violin Fairy – 978-1-40830-027-5
Sadie the Saxophone Fairy – 978-1-40830-032-9

The Magical Animal Fairies

Ashley the Dragon Fairy – 978-1-40830-349-8
Lara the Black Cat Fairy – 978-1-40830-350-4
Erin the Firebird Fairy – 978-1-40830-351-1
Rihanna the Seahorse Fairy – 978-1-40830-352-8
Sophia the Snow Swan Fairy – 978-140830-353-5
Leona the Unicorn Fairy – 978-1-40830-354-2
Caitlin the Ice Bear Fairy – 978-1-40830-355-9

The Ocean Fairies

Ally the Dolphin Fairy – 978-1-40830-815-8
Amelie the Seal Fairy – 978-1-40830-816-5
Pia the Penguin Fairy – 978-1-40830-817-2
Stephanie the Starfish Fairy – 978-1-40830-819-6
Tess the Sea Turtle Fairy – 978-1-40830-818-9
Whitney the Whale Fairy – 978-1-40830-820-2
Courtney the Clown Fish Fairy – 978-1-40830-821-9

The Green Fairies
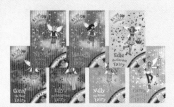

Nicole the Beach Fairy – 978-1-40830-474-7
Isabella the Air Fairy – 978-1-40830-475-4
Edie the Garden Fairy – 978-1-40830-476-1
Coral the Reef Fairy – 978-1-40830-477-8
Lily the Rainforest Fairy – 978-1-40830-478-5
Milly the River Fairy – 978-1-40830-480-8
Carrie the Snow Cap Fairy – 978-1-40830-479-2

The Twilight Fairies

Ava the Sunset Fairy – 978-1-40830-906-3
Lexi the Firefly Fairy – 978-1-40830-907-0
Zara the Starlight Fairy – 978-1-40830-908-7
Morgan the Midnight Fairy – 978-1-40830-909-4
Yasmin the Night Owl Fairy – 978-1-40830-910-0
Maisie the Moonbeam Fairy – 978-1-40830-911-7
Sabrina the Sweet Dreams Fairy – 978-1-40830-912-4

The Specials

All priced at £3.99. Holiday Specials are priced at £5.99. Orchard Books are available from all good bookshops, or can be ordered from: www.orchardbooks.co.uk, or telephone 01235 827702, or fax 01235 827703.

Holly the Christmas Fairy – 978-1-84362-661-9
Summer the Holiday Fairy – 978-184362-960-3
Stella the Star Fairy – 978-1-84616-919-9
Kylie the Carnival Fairy – 978-1-84616-175-9
Paige the Pantomine Fairy – 978-1-84616-209-1
Flora the Fancy Dress Fairy – 978-1-84616-505-4
Chrissie the Wish Fairy – 978-1-84616-506-1
Shannon the Ocean Fairy – 978-1-40830-025-1
Gabriella the Snow Kingdom Fairy – 978-1-40830-034-3
Mia the Bridesmaid Fairy – 978-1-40830-348-1
Destiny the Pop Star Fairy – 978-1-40830-473-0
Juliet the Valentine Fairy – 978-1-40831-135-6
Belle the Birthday Fairy – 978-1-40830-810-3
Trixie the Halloweeen Fairy – 978-1-40831-138-7

Choose Your Own Magic titles

Ruby the Red Fairy – 978-1-40830-789-2
Katie and the Missing Kitten – 978-1-40830-812-7